THE DEVIL DIED AT MIDNIGHT

A JOSS JAX MYSTERY

CHERYL BRADSHAW

NEW YORK TIMES BESTSELLING AUTHOR

D1518616

First US edition March 2017
Copyright © 2017 by Cheryl Bradshaw
Cover Design Copyright 2017 © Indie Designz
All rights reserved.
ISBN: 1544009097
ISBN: 978-1544009094

To Susan Payne
For teaching me to follow my bliss, pushing me to achieve my dreams, and for always believing in me. I miss you.

"The dogmas of the quiet past are inadequate to the stormy present. The occasion is piled high with difficulty, and we must rise — with the occasion. As our case is new, so we must think anew, and act anew."

—Abraham Lincoln

CHAPTER 1

ALEXANDRA WESTON FIDDLED WITH THE CAP ON HER black Sharpie pen, popping it off and on while gazing out the window at the patchy drops of rain bleeding from a bleak, overcast sky. It was December. And it was cold. Not frigid cold, but cold enough.

One hour and forty-two minutes had passed since her book signing began at Bienville Street Bookstore. She was aware of the exact time because the shop had a square metal clock the size of a card table hanging from the center of the wall on the second floor. And because she was in the home stretch, the last eighteen minutes of the final stop of her book tour.

A crooked smile broadened across Alexandra's face just thinking of how good it felt to be home again. *Home.* The word itself enveloped her like the warmth of a wool blanket.

It was Alexandra's first night back in New Orleans, and she knew exactly how she would spend it—at home with her daughter, sharing a full plate of Louisiana crab cakes and a celebratory bottle of wine. After weeks spent in three-inch heels, dresses one or two sizes too small, and strained smiles while she forced herself to answer the same tedious, repetitive fan questions over and over again, she deserved an evening of indulgence. She also deserved a good night's sleep, but rest—the "knock you on your ass so you feel like a million bucks the next morning" kind—didn't come easily. Not since the nightmares had started again.

Soon her life would change forever.

Soon the world would know the truth.

She welcomed it and feared it at the same time.

For now, she had a few more copies of her newest book to sign.

Alexandra's original true-crime story, *The Devil Died at Midnight*, based on the life of serial killer Elias Pratt, was an instant hit when it had first released twenty-five years earlier in 1990. The book propelled to the top of the *New York Times* bestsellers list, where it remained for eight consecutive weeks. She wasn't surprised. People had insatiable appetites for dissecting the minds of notorious killers, especially when it came to the dashing, debonair Elias, whose conviction was surrounded by controversy. Everyone believed he was guilty, but not everyone believed he deserved the death penalty.

A year earlier, her agent, Barbara Berry had pitched Alexandra an idea to revive Elias's story. Her publisher was interested in releasing a special twenty-five year edition of Elias Pratt's story, a "where are they now" look at his victims and their families.

"It will be simple," Barbara had said. "All you have to do is conduct a few interviews, tack a few brief chapters onto the original book, add a few new, never-before-seen photos, go on a short book tour, then sit back and collect royalties. Easy peasy."

To Alexandra, there was nothing easy about it. And the timing was bad. She had other ideas. She didn't want this book to spoil them. When she declined a second time, Barbara offered an ultimatum. Either she agreed to what the publisher wanted or the publishing house would release the amended version using another author: up-and-coming true-crime writer and television host Joss Jax.

Joss flipping Jax?

Even with Joss's recent success, the mere thought of her researching Elias's story was offensive. Joss was a child compared to her. Joss didn't *know* Elias. Alexandra did. And Alexandra wasn't about to allow Joss the satisfaction of poaching her own story. So she did a few interviews, wrote a few updates, and rebranded the title, which was now called *The Devil Wakes.*

Overall, her career had been a success, even if it hadn't started out that way. While her friends' parents praised the achievements of their own daughters, Alexandra's mother had always been unsupportive. Her *Westons never amount to anything* attitude led to years of self-doubt, especially in the early days, where rejections were a frequent occurrence. "You're a Weston," her mother had said. "Westons aren't authors, or lawyers, or doctors, or anything fancy like that. We're ordinary, hard-working people. Best you accept it now than face years of disappointment trying to be someone you're not."

Alexandra could have accepted her mother's words, could have suffocated and cowered from the years spent dealing with her mother's cruelty and abuse, but she didn't. Instead, she let the words wash over her, allowing them to fuel her drive and determination to succeed. Now when her deceased mother's voice rang in her ear, she smiled, knowing her mother had been wrong, and wishing her mother had been alive long enough to realize it.

With five minutes remaining before the book signing concluded, Alexandra shifted her focus to the last two people in line. One man, one woman. The woman was familiar, in her thirties, wearing a violet zip-up hoodie, a beanie on her head, boot-cut jeans, and gray Converse shoes. The majority of her hair was tucked behind the beanie, but a few violet wisps peeked through, just enough to reveal her identity.

The man standing in front of the woman was pushing fifty and had a receding hairline to prove it. Alexandra waved him over. He approached the table like a timid mouse and grinned, showing off a giant monstrosity of a thing—a snaggletooth jutting from the upper left side of his mouth. Alexandra averted her eyes, pretended she hadn't noticed the dental disaster. She doubted it worked. She was gifted at playing it cool, but this was a bit much.

Alexandra reached for the book he was holding and said, "Hello."

The man tossed the book onto the table instead of into her hand, pushing his pointer finger onto the center of the cover and sliding it across the table in her direction. She flipped it open to the title page, watched him rub his hands together in rapid motion like an overexcited child on his birthday.

"Is it true?" he asked, eyes wide, glossy.

She knew what was coming next, of course. The same comment that *always* came next. Still, she indulged it like she'd done so many times before. "Is *what* true?"

"Were you really there when Elias fried in the electric chair? Did you see it? Did you watch?"

"Yes."

The man was practically salivating now. "And he looked you in the eye before he died?"

Again, she answered, "Yes."

Even sitting here now, in front of a man she'd never met, his eyes bugging out, she could still picture Elias's death like it happened only yesterday.

"What was it like to be there? I mean, watching the life get sucked out of him must have been wicked cool."

Wicked?

Yes.

Cool?

Not so much.

"What's your name?" she asked.

"Lester."

She signed the paperback and handed it to him. "Well, Lester, the answers to all your questions are in the book."

He clutched the autographed copy in both hands, pressed it to his chest, and stood there, hovering over her like a cat ready to pounce. "It's just so great to meet you in person, to meet the woman who spent so many years of her life getting close to Elias Pratt, getting to know all the killers you've interviewed in your lifetime."

Over the past several weeks, Alexandra had seen far too many of Lester's kind—people only interested in meeting her because they assumed she'd had an intimate bond with Elias. Most fans were normal, average, exhibiting a harmless curiosity in Elias's story. Then there were the others, cultish, those in awe of serial killers. People like Lester. These fans were of a certain breed, like test-tube rats, holding Elias on a pedestal that even death couldn't decimate.

"You *were* close to Elias, weren't you?" Lester pressed.

"I wasn't *close* to Mr. Pratt," she replied. "Getting to know him was purely for the sake of research for the book. Nothing more."

He squinted one eye, curving his lips into a crooked grin. "I bet that's what you tell everyone, huh? Does anyone actually *believe* that garbage?"

Alexandra's heart pulsed inside her chest, fast and heavy. Dut-dum. Dut-dum. "Excuse me?"

He licked his lips, leaned in even closer, his fevered breath moistening her cheek. "How 'bout I buy you a drink tonight, maybe get to know you better? Talk some more about this book of yours. You like that?"

Alexandra stroked her chin, a rehearsed gesture aimed at the security guard standing twenty feet away: *we have a live one*. A fanatic. A freak alert. But before the guard shuffled his considerable girth in her direction, the woman standing behind Lester stepped forward, tapping him on the shoulder. "How about you back the hell off Mrs. Weston?"

Lester didn't move. His eyes remained fixed on Alexandra.

"Now," the woman said.

"Wasn't talkin' to you," he grunted.

"Your book is signed, and the store is about to close," the woman continued. "Time for you to leave."

The man grimaced then arced his body around. "This conversation don't concern you, ma'am. Mind your business."

The woman crossed her arms in front of her, bending her head to the side like she was toying with him in the same way he'd just toyed with Alexandra. "Let me put it to you in a way you can understand, m'kay? You have five seconds to back away from Mrs. Weston's table and leave the store, or I'll show you just how *concerned* I can be."

Alexandra glanced at the store's security guard once more, an oafish, overweight man named Louis, who, up to now, had exhibited no bite in his bark whatsoever. Panting, Louis reached Alexandra's desk and raised a brow, blinking at her as if his few brain cells couldn't determine what he was supposed to do next—step in or hold off.

Lester flattened a hand and thrust it against the woman's shoulder. "*I* don't have to go *nowhere.*"

Alexandra smacked the security guard's chest with the back of her hand. "Don't just stand there, you idiot. *Do* something!"

A confused Louis reached for Lester, but his hand didn't connect before the woman's hand did. With a single swoop she wrenched Lester's arm behind his body, smacking his face into the wall.

"Move an inch and your arm gets broken," the woman said.

A young, angel-faced male employee observing the commotion from across the room leapt into the scene. He looked at the woman who'd subdued Lester and squeaked, "Excuse me, what's going on here? You need to let the man go or I'll call the cops."

"Call them. Right now." The woman tipped a head toward Louis. "And we're going to need an actual cop, not mall security. Got it?"

The employee's jaw gaped open. Louis's jaw gaped open.

"You heard the lady," Alexandra chimed in. "The man she's restraining verbally assaulted *me* and then physically attacked *her*. Don't just stand there gawking. Make the damned call!"

The employee muttered an apology in Alexandra's direction and dashed away. Minutes later, the police arrived, asking a series of questions before placing zip-ties on Lester's wrists and carting him away. Conflict over, the woman stepped up to the table.

Alexandra accepted the book from the woman's hands, set it on the table, and smiled at the woman in front of her. "It's nice to finally meet you in person, Miss Jax."

Joss Jax pulled the beanie off her head, her dark locks falling around her shoulders. She combed her fingers through her hair. "Are you sure about that?"

Alexandra laughed. "Of course. We're fellow authors. Though you did make a play for Elias's story."

"I was suggested as an alternative if you refused. I wasn't interested. They only mentioned it to get you focused. It looks like it worked."

She was witty and sharp, more personable than Alexandra expected. "I've seen your show."

"How do you like it so far?"

"It's not bad, but then, I'd watch those investigative shows all day if I could."

"To be honest, I was surprised they hired me to host."

"Why?"

"I'm a writer. I know little about television."

"How did you get the job then?"

"The producers heard I was a fan of the network. They were looking for a public figure with a general knowledge of forensics."

"You definitely look the part. You're edgy. Likeable. Captivating with those dark eyes of yours. I'm sure you appeal to their demographic." Alexandra signed Joss's book, handed it back to her, grabbed the few remaining books off the table, and shoved them inside a plastic bin on the floor. "I appreciate you coming to my aid tonight."

"I hope this kind of thing doesn't happen often."

Alexandra swished a hand through the air. "Not usually. You?"

"Not much."

"I had a young stick of a thing follow me back to my hotel room once after a signing. She was harmless. Just an overzealous fan obsessed with the man I was writing about at the time. I don't get creeps like this Lester fellow often. He's crazy, but not the *I'm here to kill you* kind of crazy."

Joss laughed. "I heard you're retiring soon."

"It's true. I don't have a passion for writing like I once did."

Joss raised the book in the air. "Is this your last book then?"

Alexandra's eyes lingered on Joss for a few seconds. Was she making general conversation or fishing for something else? "What brings you to New Orleans?"

"The show is on hiatus. I thought I'd get away for a while."

"How long are you here?"

"A few more days."

Alexandra reached into her handbag, pulled out a piece of paper and a pen. "Thanks again for standing up for me tonight. Here's my home address. If you have some time tomorrow, why don't you stop by? My daughter Chelsea would love to meet you. She's seen every episode of your show."

Joss didn't appear to be listening. She was focused on Alexandra's hands. "Are you all right?"

"Of course. Why wouldn't I be?"

"Your hands, they're shaking."

Alexandra looked down. Joss was right. Her hands were trembling. She placed them on her lap, out of sight. "I'm just a bit jittery. Perhaps it's all the coffee I've had."

"Or what Lester put you through."

Either excuse was plausible, except for one thing.

Alexandra's face felt numb, her body weak, her perfect vision blurred and fuzzy.

She didn't know what caused it exactly.

She only knew something wasn't right.

CHAPTER 2

ALEXANDRA NEEDED TO PEE. SHE ALSO SUFFERED from an intense, churning pressure in her abdomen, making her feel as though she needed to vomit. With Joss gone, she located a restroom adjacent to the children's book section of the store and entered the second of three bathroom stalls. In addition to the nausea, the numbness in her face had spread, and her heart was racing.

A minute later, the bathroom door opened and closed.

And then ... silence.

No one entered the stall on either side of her.

No one turned the faucet on.

But a woman *was* there.

Lurking.

Alexandra could hear her breathing.

Slow. Heavy. Impatient breaths.

Alexandra heard a distinct click, like the door to the bathroom had been bolted. She flushed the toilet, flipped the latch on the metal stall door, and pushed it open, shocked to find the other occupant in the room wasn't a woman like she'd assumed—it was a man. At least she thought it was a man. He wore baggy clothes, leather gloves, and a plain, dingy, gray beanie on his head. His face was masked with a full beard, and he wore a pair of dark, round, mirrored glasses.

His gloved hands were shaking.

Her bare hands were too.

Thinking of the ordeal she'd just had with Lester, a single thought crossed her mind: *not this shit again.*

"I believe you have the wrong restroom," she said. "This is the ladies'."

He grunted a laugh, took a step forward.

She took two steps back.

He stepped forward again. The two continued the dance until Alexandra's back was against the wall. There was no place left to go.

"I'm going to have to ask you to back away," she said. "Right now. Or—"

Her mouth snapped shut when the silver tip of a knife's blade was pressed to the center of her neck.

Stay calm. Stay strong. No need to panic. He's a crazed fan. You've dealt with them before. You'll deal with them again. Give him what he wants, and he'll leave.

"Who are you?" she demanded.

Her attacker didn't move, remained silent.

"Why are you doing this?" she continued. "What do you want? Money? I never carry cash with me at these things. If you think you can—"

"Do you regret it?"

His voice was monotone.

Robotic.

It didn't sound real.

"Do I regret *what?*" Alexandra asked. "How could I possibly answer that when I have no idea who you are or what I'm supposed to be regretting."

"You know *exactly* what I mean. Apologize for all the lives you've ruined. Say you're sorry."

"I'm *sorry?*"

"Is this a joke? Is it funny to you?!"

She gnawed on her lower lip, blinked the tears away, composed herself, tried again. "I'm … I'm … sorry. Truly, I am. I never meant to offend you. Please, you must believe me. I didn't mean to offend you … or anyone."

"And your regrets? What about your regrets?"

"Of course. I have many regrets. A lifetime of them. Who doesn't?"

"A lifetime of *lies* is what you have. Lies and secrets."

The tip of the blade poked at her throat, piercing the skin. It wasn't much. No more than a sixteenth of an inch. Just enough for a single line of blood to trail down her neck, staining her shirt.

"Tell me what you want me to do, and I'll do it," she pleaded.

The man leaned forward, his steamy breath pulsing a wave of goose bumps along Alexandra's milky skin. The closeness between them sparked an air of familiarity.

"You think I'm stupid?" he said. "You don't even know what you're apologizing for, do you?"

She didn't. And it wasn't like she could cater an apology specifically for him. How could she without knowing what she'd done to offend him in the first place?

Unless …

No.

It couldn't be.

Hardly anyone knew about the book.

And yet …

"Put the knife down," she said. "I'm sure we can work something out. Let's talk about this. Please. I'll do anything. I have a family."

Why did I just mention my family?

"I know."

"Don't you touch them! Don't you dare touch them! You hear me?"

The nausea pulsed through her in a quick, unstoppable wave, followed by a complete loss of control. The man jerked the knife away from her neck, and she slumped to the floor, unscathed. He wasn't going to stab her.

Everything made sense now.

The nausea.

The shaking.

Her attacker's fake voice.

She hadn't been stabbed. She'd been poisoned.

Lying on the filthy bathroom floor, feeling the last few moments of her life ebbing away, she stole one last glance at her attacker.

He wasn't just vaguely familiar.

She knew him.

CHAPTER 3

The Next Morning

NEW ORLEANS WAS ONE OF THOSE PLACES I KNEW I'd never fully appreciate until I experienced it firsthand. No amount of personal stories or episodes of *Treme* could convey the flavor of a city so rich in historic culture as seeing it in person could.

I was staying at an upscale hotel in the French Quarter, which could only be described as interesting. The area, not the hotel. I use the word interesting because, at certain times of the day, Bourbon Street and its adjoining cross streets emitted a distinct odor, a foul smell, like someone had just taken a giant piss in a frying pan and set it on a stove over high heat.

Foul smell aside, the city drew me in, pumping a healthy dose of nostalgia through my veins from the moment the plane touched down, and it was easy to see why the Big Easy was a tourist phenomenon. The jubilant jazz music wafting through the streets was unparalleled to anything I'd experienced before. And I'd seen and heard plenty in my thirty-eight years.

I was kicked back on the bed, scouring through a magazine for freefall skydiving companies, when Finch walked in. Finch was actually his surname. His first name was Gregory, but when I'd read his full name aloud two years earlier during his job interview, he'd corrected me saying, "It's not Gregory. It's Greg." I preferred Gregory, so now he was Finch.

Finch could be described as the Clark Kent of the military. Or retired military, I should say. On the outside, his forty-five-year-old schoolboy charm and simple, understated style made him appear sweet and amiable. Beneath the façade, however, was a trim, toned man who was loyal, perceptive, and didn't screw around. After twenty years of faithful service in a special ops unit in the military, he'd returned home to find his not-so-loving wife six-months pregnant. Only problem? He hadn't seen her in nine. Broken and lost, he filed for divorce and walked out of her life forever. Three weeks later, he walked into mine.

Finch plopped down on the bed next to me, pressing a crooked finger to the middle of his eyeglasses, centering them on the bridge of his nose again.

"I have no idea how you see out of those things," I said.

"What do you mean?" he replied. "I see just fine."

I set the magazine I was perusing on my lap and leaned forward, sweeping a few of his stick-straight, blond locks to the side with my finger. "Your bangs almost touch the tip of your nose. It's like hair gone wild. I know you wanted a change from the military cut, but this is getting a bit extreme, don't you think? I can't even see your eyes sometimes when you're talking to me."

He frowned, which I suspected had little to do with my comment and more to do with something else.

"What's bugging you?" I asked.

"What?"

"The look on your face. Something's wrong."

"Your mother called."

"Again?"

He nodded. "Third time this week. If you'd call her back, maybe she'd stop calling *me*."

"It's easier if she calls you. Then I don't have to talk to her."

"I'm your bodyguard, not your personal assistant."

I laughed. "She doesn't see the difference."

"Can you just call her?"

"I will."

"When?"

I shrugged. "I don't know. Soon."

Finch raised a brow. "I don't believe you."

Truth was, I didn't believe me either. I'd avoided her calls for two weeks. I knew what she wanted. The same thing she'd wanted for the past month. My answer was the same as the last time I talked to her. I didn't see the point in rehashing it. "I'll call her. I just haven't made a decision yet."

"You're running out of time."

I sighed. "I know. I know. Can we talk about something else? *Anything* else?"

"Sure, if you promise to call her."

"I'll call her," I said. "Tomorrow."

He crossed his arms. "Today, Joss."

"Fine. Today."

"And don't ditch out on me again, okay?"

"You mean last night? I wore a hat."

"A hat doesn't protect you."

"It does if I'm not recognized."

He sighed. "You need to let me do what I was hired to do. Otherwise, there's no point in me being on this trip."

"I asked you if you wanted time off. You didn't."

I'd grown so used to his shadow I'd forgotten how it felt not having him around. The night before, when I'd heard about Alexandra's book signing, he was asleep. I decided I was fine on my own, and I slipped out. I arrived back at the room an hour later and found him awake and unhappy. Very unhappy.

My attention shifted to a newswoman on TV. I swore she'd just uttered something about Alexandra Weston being found dead in a bookstore bathroom. Frantic to learn more, I smoothed a hand across the bedspread, fishing for the remote. "Where's the control for the TV? Have you seen it?"

Finch glanced around, then lifted his right butt cheek. He reached down, grabbed the remote control, and handed it to me. A wide grin spread across his face. "Guess I sat on it. Brings a whole new meaning to the phrase 'pain in the ass,' doesn't it?"

He laughed. I shook my head, smacked him on the arm with the remote, and increased the volume on the television just in time to hear the news anchor say, "Today the world is reeling from the loss of bestselling true-crime author Alexandra Weston, who was found dead inside a restroom last night at Bienville Street Bookstore. We're still waiting on more information from the police."

CHAPTER 4

A HEAVY RAPPING SOUNDED FROM THE OPPOSITE side of my hotel room door.

"I'll get it," Finch said.

I rose from the bed. "It's okay. I got it."

He grimaced, racing me to the door.

I glanced out the peephole at two uniformed officers in the hallway. One male, one female. The female glared straight at the hole like she was keenly aware of my eyeball peering at her from the opposite side. I cracked the door just enough to wedge my body into the opening and directed my attention to the woman. Her chestnut-colored hair was pulled back into a taut ponytail. And when I say taut, the ponytail was so tight it looked like her face had just been nipped *and* tucked. She was a few inches shorter than I was, around five foot seven, and had an interesting shape—chicken legs from the knee down and thunder thighs on top, giving her lower half the appearance of a human candy corn.

She frowned, her plain, dull eyes boring into mine.

"Can I help you?" I asked.

"Joss Jax?"

"Yes?"

"I'm Officer Blunt, and this is Officer Parks."

Officer *Blunt*.

The shoe fit perfectly.

I switched my gaze to Parks. He was tall and bald. Lanky. He looked young and green, like it was his first week on the job. He extended a hand toward me. Blunt swatted it away.

"You don't need to shake the woman's hand, Parks," she scolded. "We're here to ask questions, not to get better acquainted."

"Oh," he said, his eyes darting to the floor. "Sorry. It's just … I'm a big fan. A big, *big* fan. I've never missed an episode of your show, Miss Jax. And I've read most of your books."

I stuck my hand out to him, and he accepted it. "Call me Joss."

He beamed. Officer Blunt rolled her eyes and tried to push the hotel room door forward, expecting me to allow her access just because she was in uniform and wanted in. I maintained my position. Golden tickets didn't come this easily. Not with me.

"Can we come in?" she asked.

It was more of an expectation than a query.

"Why?" I asked.

"We need to talk to you about Alexandra Weston."

"So go ahead and talk."

"Are you aware of what's happened?"

"Vaguely," I said. "I just saw the story on the news."

"She was found dead last night at the bookstore on Bienville," Parks said. "Looks like she may have been murdered."

Blunt gave him a sharp sideways glance, and he resumed staring at the floor.

"You witnessed a scuff-up last night between Alexandra Weston and Lester Barnes, right?" Blunt asked.

"I did. What about it?"

She moved a hand to her hip. "What is it with you, responding to all of my questions with questions?"

"I'm just trying to move this along."

"There's no need to get snippy."

"I'm not getting *snippy*," I said. "If I was, you'd have no problem understanding the difference."

She glared at me like she wanted to put a bullet between my eyes.

"Look, I'd like to ask you a few questions," she said. "And I'd rather do it inside your room instead of in the hallway where any Joe Blow with nothing better to do is privy to our conversation. If that isn't to your liking, you can come with me, and we'll have this conversation elsewhere."

I assumed "elsewhere" was code for the police department, or whatever they called it here. Technically, she had no warrant, which meant I had every right to slam the door in her face if I wanted. She wasn't taking me anywhere. I was a person of interest, not a suspect. She needed *me*, not the other way around.

Still, I had to admit, I was curious. I wondered what other information might slip from Officer Parks's mouth if I let them in. I pulled the door all the way open, allowing both officers inside. In the far corner, next to a window overlooking a courtyard with a fifteen-foot marble fountain in the middle, the four of us sat down.

Blunt thumbed at Finch. "Who's this, your boyfriend?"

Finch cupped a hand over his month, half-coughed, half-laughed. "Uh, no."

"He works for me," I said.

"In what capacity?"

"Why does it matter?" I asked.

"I'm her bodyguard," Finch offered.

Thinking it was a joke, Blunt snapped her head back, snorted.

Parks nudged her. "I told you. She's on TV. Hosts a homicide show. *Murderous Minds*. She's famous. Famous people have bodyguards all the time."

Blunt clicked the top of her ballpoint pen, unfazed. "Huh. Well, I've never seen the show. I don't need to watch things like that. I deal with homicide in real life. What time did you arrive at the bookstore last night?"

I told her.

"And what time did you leave?"

I told her that too.

"Who else was present while you were there?"

"A few employees, Lester Barnes, Alexandra Weston, and a security guy named Louis."

"Are you sure you didn't see anyone else lurking around?"

I shook my head. "The store was about to close."

"I read what you said about Lester in the statement you gave to police. You restrained him. Why didn't you let the security guard handle the situation?"

I grinned. "The guy moved like his feet were stuck in blocks of cement. He was in no hurry to come to her aid."

"Interesting. Why not?"

"Probably because his considerable girth would have made him exert more energy than he thought it was worth, and because it was a crappy, hourly paid job. How would I know? I could see she was in trouble. I was close, so I stepped in. I thought I was doing her a favor. The guy was nuts."

"Funny."

"What is?" I asked.

"Lester said the same thing about you."

"Of course he did," I snapped.

"You're not surprised?"

"Should I be?"

"Maybe."

I leaned back, crossed one leg over the other. "I'd like to help you. I'm a big fan of Alexandra Weston and her books. With the exception of the one she signed for me last night, I've read everything she's written."

"How nice. After Lester was escorted from the store, did you talk with her?"

"Briefly."

"What about?"

"Her book," I said. "Writing. My job."

"Why would you talk about your job?"

I sighed. This was getting ridiculous. "Alexandra Weston is a fellow author who writes in the same genre I do."

Blunt nodded. "So you … know her."

"I know who she is, yes. We aren't buddies. Last night was the first time we've met."

"Did she say anything significant to you when you saw her?"

"No."

"Did she seem agitated or worried about anything?"

I mulled the question over for a moment. There were pros and cons involved with gratuitous oversharing with police. "She told me Lester wasn't the first person who'd ever harassed her."

Blunt leaned in. "What were her *exact* words?"

"She said a woman had followed her back to her hotel room after a signing once. The woman was harmless, just a fan obsessed with a book she'd written."

"And?"

"She said she'd run into a few creeps like Lester over the years."

"She give you any names? Locations where she may have been harassed?"

I shook my head. "Honestly, she talked about it like it was no big deal."

"How did the visit end?"

"She signed my book, invited me to stop by her house while I was here so I could meet her daughter."

"Then what?"

"I left," I said.

"Where did you go?"

"If you're asking where I was at the time Alexandra Weston died, I'd need to know the exact time her death occurred."

I knew Blunt wouldn't give it to me, and any hope I had of Parks blurting out the answer was dashed when Blunt glared at him like she'd saw his head off if he spoke a word.

"After you left the bookstore, where did you go?"

"I returned back here," I said.

"Can anyone confirm it?"

"I don't need anyone to *confirm* it. That's what happened."

Blunt tapped a plain, un-manicured fingernail on the table.

"How did she die?" I asked.

"Can't say," Blunt replied.

"That *is* why you're asking these questions, right? The way she died must relate to you considering me as a person of interest."

"Let's stick to the question I asked you—the one you didn't answer. Did anyone see you arrive back at the hotel?"

"Lots of people."

"Such as?"

Finch leaned back in the chair, entwined his fingers behind his head. "Me. I was here when she got back."

Blunt shifted her focus. "*You?* You weren't with her at the bookstore?"

He frowned at me. "Unfortunately, no."

"Just what kind of bodyguard work do you do for her that has you waiting in her hotel room for her to return?"

"The none-of-your-business kind," he replied.

"What time did Miss Jax arrive back at the hotel?"

"Somewhere around nine forty-five, I guess."

"You *guess* or you know?"

"You're wasting your time, officer," I said. "I allowed you inside my hotel room as a courtesy. If you're going to turn this into an interrogation, you won't like the end result."

Blunt snapped her notebook shut and stood. "Why are you here, in New Orleans?"

"Why does anyone come to New Orleans?"

Blunt prodded Parks with a finger, jerked her head toward the door. He stood like a trained animal and walked in that direction. She followed, stepped into the hall with him, and turned. "How much longer are you staying?"

"I haven't decided yet," I said. "Why?"

She shrugged. "No reason."

I resisted the urge to say anything more and closed the door.

Of course there was a reason.

There always was.

CHAPTER 5

"WE'RE NOT SKYDIVING TODAY, ARE WE?" FINCH ASKED. "You want to find out what happened to the Weston lady. Am I right?"

"'No' to your first question," I said, "and 'yes' to your second. If she *was* murdered, I want to know why."

"You don't *want* to know, Joss. You *need* to know. There's a difference."

He was right. I did need to know. My curiosity wouldn't let it drop.

Finch opened his mouth, and I prepared for the incoming lecture about letting the police do the work. I wasn't a cop. I was the host of a television show by day and a writer with semi-decent forensic knowledge by night.

"I won't bother trying to talk you out of whatever you feel you need to do," he said. "You're going to do what you want, no matter what I say."

He was right about *that* too.

"At least give me today and tomorrow," I said. "Let me dig around a bit. If I don't find anything, we'll resume all death-defying activities as planned. Okay?"

"You're still calling your mom, right?" he asked.

"When I have time, yes."

He gave me his *I'm disappointed* look. "Joss."

"Later on, okay?"

"Not later on. Now. I'm not filtering any more calls from her. Like I said, it's not what you pay me to do."

"I know it isn't. But you don't just *work* for me, Finch. We're friends."

He handed me the phone. "Friends don't make other friends deal with their own mothers."

I took the phone, winked. "Oh, come on. Some friends do."

He walked to the adjoining door dividing our two rooms and stepped into his, shutting the door behind him. I sighed, thought about how much I needed a strong sedative right about now, and dialed the number. My mother picked up on the first ring, almost like she'd expected the call.

"Well, well," she began, "look who finally made time to talk to her mother."

"Hi, Mom."

"Did Finchie tell you I've been calling?"

"His name is Finch."

"Whatever. Did he?"

"He did."

"And?"

"This is me calling you back," I said.

"How are you doing?"

"Fine."

"I mean, how are you doing *today*?"

"Busy."

She blew a displeased breath into the phone. "You know what I mean, Joslyn. Today is … well, it's just … I've been thinking about you all day. That's why I called Finchie—"

"Finch, and you shouldn't be talking to him about my private life. What I choose to tell him is up to me."

"Calm down. We only talked about your cousin's wedding. Seems to me like you're struggling today, and I just want you to know I'm here if you need me."

"I can't do this, Mom. I can't talk to you if we're going to talk about the past. I said I was fine, and I am."

"Fine" equaled occupying the rest of today with any activity that didn't require use of my brain.

"Are you coming to Clay and Courtney's wedding or not? It's next weekend."

"I know. I haven't decided yet."

"Why not? You've known about it for several months now. You're not filming right now, and whatever book project you're working on, I'm sure you can take a break."

"Give me the rest of the week to decide, Mom. Okay?"

"Come home, Joslyn. Please. We all miss you. Everyone wants to see you."

Not everyone.

"I will. I just don't know if it will be before the wedding."

She sighed the way she usually did when she didn't get what she wanted. "Listen, honey, I know it's hard coming back here after what happened. Have you ever thought about how good it might feel to face everyone at the wedding? It's been five years, Joslyn. Everyone has moved on. Everyone except you."

"Clay is the brother of my ex. I *doubt* he's moved on."

Another sigh. Much deeper this time. "Maybe if you talk to your father ... hold on and I'll get him."

"Wait, Mom. Don't. I have to go."

"What? Why? We've only just started talking."

"I know, and I'm sorry," I said. "I'll call you again later, okay?"

"Today?"

"If I can. I'm assisting the police with a local investigation."

"What investigation? What's going on?"

"I'll tell you all about it next time we talk. Tell Dad I love him and give my love to the family. I love you, and I'll see you soon. I promise. Bye."

I pressed the end button on the phone before she had the chance to utter another word and embraced the swelling ball of guilt festering inside me.

Finch poked his head back in. "How'd it go?"

I turned away. "Did you ... umm, could you hear me?"

"Some. You sound so different when you to talk to her."

"In what way?"

"You don't sound like yourself. The Joss I know is fearless. Last week, you jumped from a plane. Last month, you swam with sharks. Last—"

"This is different."

"Why? Because she's your mother?"

"It has nothing to do with her. And, to be honest, it has nothing to do with the wedding either. Well, almost nothing."

He crossed his arms, leaned against the wall. "What happened five years ago?"

He *was* listening.

"Let's talk about it another time, okay?"

He leaned against the doorway. "You remember when I interviewed with you, what you asked me?"

"I asked you a lot of things. I needed to be sure you were the right person for the job."

"The last thing you asked me was what made me leave Tennessee and travel to California to work for you."

"I remember," I said.

"I could have said anything. I could have told you what I thought you wanted to hear. I didn't. We were strangers, and still, I laid it all out for you—my wife's infidelity, the baby, all of it. I knew it could have cost me the job. I told you anyway."

"Your honesty was one of the things that won me over, Finch. It built trust between us."

"Trust goes both ways. You said it yourself. I don't just work for you. We're friends."

I smiled. "I know we are."

"If you want to talk to me about anything, you always can."

I smiled. "Thank you. It means a lot to me. It really does."

"And if you don't want to go to this wedding, don't go. She'll get over it."

I knew she would.

The question was … would I?

CHAPTER 6

THE DETAILS OF ALEXANDRA WESTON'S DEATH WERE scant at best. The news channels had little to go on, and as a result, they kept broadcasting the same alleged bits of information they'd received in a repetitive loop. The police hadn't made a public statement. I wanted to know why and decided to take my query straight to the superintendent of police.

I hadn't made it very far inside the department walls before Blunt stopped me.

Hands on hips, she said, "What are *you* doing here?"

"I came to speak to the superintendent."

"About what?"

"Alexandra Weston."

"Why? Is there something you didn't mention before?"

"No."

She laughed. "Well then, whatever it is, you can talk to me. He's busy."

I shrugged. "I'll wait."

Jaw clenched, she said, "Look, I get it. Your little real-life murder show on TV makes you feel entitled, like *you* know something we don't. Here's the thing: you're a writer reading a cue card. What we do here is *real* police work. You wouldn't know anything about it."

Finch, who stood beside me, stared at Officer Blunt and said nothing. He didn't need to. He knew what was coming.

"I know you've never seen the show," I said. "And I doubt you've read any of my books, so I'll let your ignorance about who I am and what I do slide. But before you label me, take a look at my background. I have plenty of experience."

I awaited a heated response as I watched her nostrils flare next to her raised finger. It was derailed when a plump, middle-aged man of average height appeared from a small office to my right, his bushy, uncombed head of hair taking center stage.

"You're Joss Jax, aren't you?" he asked.

I turned, nodded.

"Heard you were in town."

Blunt rolled her eyes. "Of course you heard, Herb. *I* told you."

He behaved like she wasn't there, his eyes remaining on me. "I'm Detective Murphy. The superintendent put me in charge of Alexandra Weston's case. Why don't we talk in my office?"

Gladly.

Finch and I stepped inside, and Murphy shut the door, leaving Blunt ogling me through the small office window. It wasn't hard to imagine what she was thinking.

Murphy sat down and gestured for Finch and me to do the same.

"Don't mind Blunt," he said. "She's one hell of an officer, but she's also, you know … well, forgive me for saying, but she's … uhh …"

"An unhappy woman?" I suggested.

He smirked. "I was going to go with 'a real bitch,' but hey, tact isn't my strong suit."

It wasn't mine either, but today I was feeling generous.

"You haven't released much information to the press about what happened to Alexandra Weston."

"Too early in the process. You know how it goes. We'll leak a thing or two here and there, shake a few trees, see what tumbles out." He leaned over his desk, entwining his short, chubby fingers together on top of it. "How much do you already know?"

"Not a lot. I heard she was found dead inside the bookstore bathroom a couple hours after it closed. Why did it take so long for someone to find her? Didn't anyone realize she'd never left the shop in the first place?"

"Everyone thought she slipped out, went home. From what I've heard, she wasn't much of a people person unless she wanted to be."

"There was a Chanel handbag sitting on the floor next to her chair when I was there," I said. "You're saying no one saw it or thought it was odd when she left it there?"

"She took it with her into the bathroom. It was recovered on the floor inside the stall."

"What about the pens she was handing out? There was a basket sitting on the desk during the signing. There was a bin of books too. And a mug of something—a silver container she was drinking from."

He shrugged. I continued.

"What about the surveillance tape? Didn't the bookstore have one?"

"Yes and no. They have one. It just wasn't on at the time."

"Why not?"

"One of the plugs was disconnected. Can't say yet whether it was on purpose or whether the cord just detached somehow. It's an older system, so either theory is plausible. We dusted for prints. Don't have those results yet."

"How long had the camera been broken?" I asked.

"The last recording they have is from two weeks ago."

"Two weeks, and no one noticed or cared?"

"Employees said after they hired the security guard, they hardly had any theft. Checking to see if it was working was no longer a priority."

It was hard for me to believe Louis was considered that big of a deterrent. He had the size, but lacked in mental capacity.

"The security guard was a new hire then?"

"He'd only been there three weeks. We think the killer was hiding somewhere in the store during the book signing, possibly even before, waiting for an opportunity to make his move."

"Even if that's true, how did he escape?" I asked. "The front door was locked from the inside with a key that one of the employees carried around in his pocket. I saw him lock it about ten minutes before the store closed. He'd unlocked the door to let the last few customers out, and then locked the door back up."

"We think the killer exited through the side door."

"What side door?"

"The one they use for shipments in the warehouse out back. It locks from the outside only. From the inside, anyone can push the metal bar and get out." Detective Murphy pulled a manila file from the top drawer of his desk. He flipped it open, turning the folder in my direction so I had a clear view of the photograph resting on top. An ordinary kitchen knife with a tan, wooden handle.

"We found this knife stashed inside a discarded fast-food sack in a dumpster on the opposite end of the parking lot."

"I'm guessing you didn't get any prints off it."

"Not a one. And the weirdest part is there was a very small cut on Alexandra Weston's neck, but she didn't die from a knife injury. There were no other marks on her."

"If this wasn't the cause of death, what was?"

He craned his neck, looking left and right, before saying, "Apparently Alexandra Weston wasn't feeling well. In the stall we believe she used prior to her death, it looks like she vomited. Did she seem unwell to you?"

"She never said anything to me about her stomach being upset, but she seemed a little off to me. She was shaking. I asked her about it, and she blamed it on the coffee."

When I said the word *coffee*, he blinked.

"Was she poisoned?" I asked.

"It's possible. We can't be sure of anything yet."

"Your pathologist is running a tox screen, I imagine?"

He nodded.

"Make sure you test the silver mug that was sitting on the table during the signing."

He looked at me like he wondered if I'd forgotten whom I was talking to.

"Sorry," I said. "I know you know how to do your job. How long will it be before you know something?"

He shrugged. "Not sure. Celia Burke, the forensic pathologist at the coroner's office, is running tests now. She's a little backed up at the moment though."

"Why?"

"She handles at least twenty autopsies a month."

Twenty autopsies? It had to be some kind of record. "Time to hire a second pathologist, don't you think?"

He ran a hand down his face. "Believe me. You have no idea. We're trying."

I stood, walked to the door. Finch followed.

"Have you brought in any possible suspects yet?"

"We've talked to all the employees. They're all small, scrawny things. None of them weigh more than a buck and a half. And they're … well, timid. George McFly types, pre-time travel, that is."

"Anything else I can talk you into telling me before I go?"

He leaned back, rubbed his chin. "There is *one* thing. The store's bodyguard we were just talking about. Louis. He's the only one who didn't show up for work today, but you didn't hear it from me."

CHAPTER 7

LOUIS MASSIE LIVED IN THE LOWER 9TH WARD WITH HIS
mother, a woman I was told everyone called Miss Sabine. Although
it had been almost a decade since Katrina, many neighborhoods,
including the one Louis lived in, still struggled to recover from the
devastating aftermath of the hurricane. Vacant pockets of flattened
land where homes used to be breathed a haunting reminder of the
destruction that had poisoned the area. Some people had left their
homes entirely, vowing to never look back, never return again.
Others remained, strong and resilient. Raising a torch of unfettered
bravery, they began anew. Miss Sabine was among them. On a quiet
street where only a handful of homes remained, her modest,
traditional-style dwelling with beige siding and white shutters
looked newly remodeled, transformed from its former, battered self
into a thing of beauty.

I parked at the curb, walked up a series of brick steps leading to
the house, and knocked on the door. I stood for almost a full
minute and waited. No one came. I spotted a neighbor across the
street on her porch. She was rocking back and forth on a weathered,
yellow rocking chair. A blanket was wrapped around her legs. When

she saw me, she stood, draped the blanket around her body, and walked toward me, blanket ruffling in the soft wind. She looked to be in her upper eighties, I guessed, and had short, black hair and glasses, which were too big for her face.

"'Scuse me," the woman said. "Can I help you?"

"I'm just looking for the people who live here."

"No one's home just now."

"Do you know when they'll be back?" I asked.

"Day or two, I guess. Why? What do you want with Miss Sabine?"

"I'm not here for Sabine. I'm here for Louis."

"You're the second person to come here lookin' for him today. First was the police."

"Did they talk to you?"

"Tried. I didn't care to answer the door."

Her hands moved to her hips, and she squinted, looking me over like she struggled to find even the smallest connection between Louis and me. "Louis don't live here no more, you see. Sabine kicked that boy's ass outta here. She don't want him back neither. Not until he cleans up his attitude and cleans up his life. He does nothin' but cause problems for everybody."

"When did she kick him out?"

"Been about a week ago now."

"Any idea where I can find him?"

She crossed her arms in front of her, leaned back like there was an imaginary wall behind her to hold her up, and said, "Maybe. Depends on who you are and what you're doing here."

"My name is Joss. I was in the bookstore where Louis worked the night Alexandra Weston died."

"Who?"

"Alexandra Weston, the true-crime writer."

She shrugged. "Never heard of her before."

"She was murdered the night before last, at the same place Louis worked."

The revelation failed to elicit a response.

"What does Louis have to do with it?"

"Maybe nothing. I won't know until I talk to him. He didn't show up for work today."

She didn't seem surprised.

"You don't look like you're from around here."

"I'm not."

"Where you from?"

"I work in California," I said.

"I didn't ask you where you work. I asked where you're from."

"Heber."

"Where?"

"Heber City. It's in Utah."

"Huh. Never heard of it. You a special kind of cop or somethin', sent here to investigate?"

"No."

"Then why are you poking your nose into business that ain't yours?"

"Alexandra Weston was a friend. We work in the same profession. We're both authors. I'd like to know why someone wanted to kill her."

The term *friend* was a bit loose, but it suited its purpose.

"Anyway," I continued, "I was hoping Louis saw something the night she died that could explain what happened."

She squinted one eye, looked at me like she was trying to decide whether what I'd just said was genuine. "Try Eddie Trumaine. He usually hangs out with him after work. Ask me, I bet that's where he's been stayin' too."

CHAPTER 8

THE DRIVEWAY IN FRONT OF EDDIE TRUMAINE'S DIVE of a home, if one considered a worn-down shack a home, looked like a used-car lot for misfit automobiles. Six vehicles in various phases of disrepair and decay were stacked three deep in two rows on the oil-stained asphalt driveway. Two cars were missing tires, another two had dents in various shapes and sizes, one had been spray-painted a flat, gray color, and the last was missing one of its back windows. A replacement window had been fashioned out of thick painter's plastic and black, zebra-patterned duct tape.

Not exactly what I called sweet rides.

Finch sized up the patchy, dry grass on the front lawn, the bullet-shaped holes in the white stucco on the front of the home's exterior, and the treasure trove of rundown vehicles, and said, "I'm coming with you."

I opened my mouth to object, but true to form, he was halfway to the front door before I'd even switched off the ignition. I got out, placing a hand on the hood of the gray car as I passed it. Still warm.

I knocked and heard what sounded like glass shattering on a tile floor, followed by the sound of footsteps moving rapidly in the opposite direction. Finch leapt off the porch, disappearing around the corner. I wiped the dusty windowpane with a hand, surveyed the inside of the house. Louis was on the ground, face up, not moving. I turned the handle on the door and was met with an overwhelming, foul smell of decay. I pulled the sleeve of my sweater over my hand, cupped the same hand over my nose. I gazed down at Louis. He was still dressed in his security uniform and had more than one bullet to the chest.

I didn't need to check for a pulse.

He'd been there for some time.

He wouldn't have one.

Finch flung the front door open, dragging a twenty-something-year-old kid behind him. The kid had a big, round, reddish circle around his left eye. It grew puffier by the second.

I looked at Finch. "Did you punch him?"

"It's his own fault. He wouldn't listen to me when I asked him to stop running. Now I'm confident he will."

The kid squeaked a pathetic yelp, struggling to break free. With every yowl, Finch constricted the arm he had around the kid's neck even tighter.

"Unless you wanna get choked out, stop fighting me," Finch warned. "This is your one and *only* warning."

Too paranoid to listen, the kid remained focused on his primal need for flight.

"Suit yourself," Finch said. "Up to you."

Finch increased the squeeze, and the kid's eyes started bulging.

I approached the kid. "Are you Eddie?"

"Yeah," he squealed. "Who are you? Why are you here?"

"If you calm down and stop trying to run, Finch here will let you go. All we want to know is what happened to Louis, okay? Nod if you understand."

He nodded. I exchanged glances with Finch. He didn't budge.

"At least let him talk," I said. "You're choking him."

Finch relaxed his grip.

"I didn't do nothin'," Eddie said. "What happened to Louis ... it wasn't me. I had nothin' to do with it, okay?"

"Then why is Louis dead in *your* house?" I pointed across the room. "And why's there a gun case with no guns in it? And why did you run?"

Eddie looked at the open door on the gun case. "I don't know."

The odor of rotting flesh saturated the room, filling my lungs with a nauseating feeling that almost had me expelling everything I'd eaten. "I need to get out of here. Let's talk outside."

"Hold up, Joss," Finch said. "Aren't you going to call the police first?"

I shrugged. "What for?"

"What do you mean 'what for'? So they can deal with this dead body and figure out what the hell happened to this guy."

"Time is no longer of the essence for Louis," I said. "He's already dead."

"Yes, but the sooner they examine the body, the better, right?"

"If he'd just expired, yes. My guess? He's been dead almost twenty-four hours." At the risk of upchucking all over the body, I bent down, pointed at it. "The greenish-blue color on his face and neck tells me he's been dead for at least that long." I grabbed a fork sitting beside a half-eaten chicken pot pie on the coffee table, lifted Louis's shirt a couple inches, peeked beneath it. "Yeah, the discoloration is spreading. He's been here for a while. You better start talking, Eddie."

The three of us headed outside.

On the back deck, a weather-worn chair was positioned beside a brand-new barbecue grill. Finch shoved Eddie into the chair. "Sit down. And *don't* get up."

Tiny beads of sweat dotted Eddie's forehead. "Look, I don't know who you two are. But I told you, I didn't have nothin' to do with this mess!"

"What happened to Louis?" I asked.

He shook his head. "I don't know, lady."

"Oh … kay. Tell me what you *do* know."

He stood there looking terrified. Whomever he was afraid of, it was clear we were less of a risk to him than the other person was.

"Look, there's no way out of this." I said. "If the cops haul you in, it's only going to get worse for you. Protecting the person you fear won't save you when word gets around you were interrogated by police. Even if you lie, say you didn't say anything, no one will believe you."

He raised his chin, said, "You got it all wrong. I'm not afraid of anyone. I can take care of myself."

I resisted the urge to burst out laughing. "Why did you run when we got here?"

Again he hesitated, perhaps debating his options, like he had any. "For all I know, you two are the ones who killed him."

"*You* were in the house when we got here," I said. "Which tells me you knew he was dead."

"Naw. You got it all wrong. I mean, I did see him when I got home, but I wasn't here when it happened."

"Where were you then?"

"I spent the last day with my girl. Since Louis started sleeping here, she won't stay over anymore, so I've been chillin' at her place. I just came to shower and change my clothes. I walk in, see him dead on the floor, then you two show up, and I didn't know what to do. So I ran."

"How long have you been here?"

"Ten minutes, tops."

"When was the last time you saw Louis alive?" I asked.

"Two nights ago."

"Tell us about it."

"Louis rolled up in here with a wad of cash in his hand. He was wavin' it all around, all showin' off, actin' like he'd just won the lottery or some shit."

"How much money are we talking?" I asked.

"Seven, eight C-notes, at least. Maybe more."

Confused, I looked at Finch.

"Seven or eight hundred dollars," Finch said.

"Couldn't he have just gotten paid from work and cashed the check?" I asked.

Eddie shook his head. "Naw. He don't get paid until the end of the month, and he *never* has that kind of cash even when he does get paid. He has all kinds of bills. He's dead broke."

"Where did the money come from then?"

"All he said was he was quitting his job. Found somethin' a lot more lucartive."

"You mean lucrative?" I asked.

Eddie nodded.

"Did he say who gave him the money or anything about his new job?" I asked.

Eddie scratched his head. "I mean, he just said he was movin' outta his mom's place for good."

I sensed he was still lying. He *did* know something. He just wouldn't say.

I picked my phone out of my pocket, looked at Finch. "I'm ready to make that call now."

CHAPTER 9

SEVERAL HOURS LATER, I'D DOWNED MY THIRD SHOT
of vodka, which may have actually been my fourth shot, or my
fifth. At this point, I was no longer counting. A man who'd been
eyeing me from across the bar for the last half hour mustered up
enough liquid courage to brush chicken-fingers crumbs off the front
of his plaid, button-up shirt and make his move.

He stood.

He smiled.

I smiled back.

He raised his beer bottle.

I raised my empty shot glass, thought about summoning the
barmaid for a refill.

The ice between us was officially broken.

I wondered if he'd wave next.

He didn't.

Forty-five minutes earlier, before he'd noticed me noticing him,
I watched him scan the room, turn toward the wall, wrestle his
wedding band off his finger, and shove it into his front pocket when
he thought no one was looking. It was a douche move, and it

begged the question: Why walk into the bar with it on in the first place just to take it off minutes later? The answer, of course, was a simple one. Whether or not he took it off depended on him first assessing the goods, scouting the bar to see if there was anyone worth taking it off for. I didn't know whether I felt flattered or disgusted. Actually, I felt a bit of both.

The man's face was decent in a Keebler-elf sort of way, and his broad smile reeled me in—for a moment. When the moment passed, he shoved the tips of his fingers into his jeans pockets and headed in my direction. For a man who looked like he was pushing forty, the overall package wasn't half bad. Sure his male-pattern baldness seemed to have taken a turn for the worse in recent years, even though he attempted to hide it by spiking up what sparse, brown hair he still had left. I imagined he assumed it wasn't noticeable, but denial hadn't been kind.

He reached the table and hovered over me, his eyes like a vulture, waiting for an invitation he'd never get. With all the alcohol I'd poured into my body, he probably assumed I'd be an easy lay. If so, he was mistaken.

"Hey there," he began. "Want some company?"

I didn't want company tonight, especially his, but I offered the seat beside me anyway. Whoever said chivalry was dead must not have ever hung around a bar after eleven o'clock on a weeknight.

He sat. "What's your name?"

"Lacey."

I thought about going full throttle and throwing in a last name too, but Lacey Thong was a bit too much to swallow, even for a dimwit like him.

"I'm Jordan," he said. "What are we celebrating?"

"We're not. Celebrating, I mean."

"What are we mourning then?"

I attempted a fake smile, which I assumed looked a bit like a coyote wooing a fluffy rabbit, and said nothing.

"Whoever he is, he's not worth it." He placed a hand on my wrist. "It'll be okay, you know. Been through a few breakups myself."

I resisted the urge to ask if he was referring to mistresses or wives or both. "I never said we broke up."

"You don't have to. I can see it in your eyes. I'm good at reading people."

I bit my upper lip, attempting to keep the growing urge to laugh contained.

The barmaid walked over. I flicked my shot glass in her direction so fast it almost slid off table. The confused look on her face when I said *"uno mas"* made me question whether I'd slurred my words, but she took the glass and nodded anyway. Jordan ordered a shot of whiskey. Both beverages were brought over, and we clanked our respective glasses together.

"So you're in a relationship then?" he said. "That's okay."

Of course it was.

"I'm not, and it isn't," I said.

Now he looked confused. I downed the vodka, blinking a few times at the shot glass after I set it down on the table. It looked more and more like two glasses the longer I stared at it, but I was sure the waitress had only given me the one.

Jordan licked his lips, took a moment to compose his wind-up, and then made the pitch. "So, uhh, sweetie. You wanna lift home?"

"Depends."

"On what?"

"What your intentions are."

He leaned over, whispered, "You saw me staring earlier. Hell, who wasn't? Every man in this room would give his left nut to spend an hour with your fine ass. I believe you're clear on my intentions."

Wow. What a sweet talker. How could I say no to such a fantastic offer?

"I'm clear on your intentions," I said. "But are you clear on mine?"

"I have a suite a couple blocks away. No need to rush you home, is there?" He paused then added, "I tell you what. I'll pour you another vodka or two when we get there, and we can talk."

"We're talking now."

"It's big and it's private."

He glanced at his crotch as he said the words, making me wonder if "it's big" referred to something other than his place or if it referred to his place *and* the growing erection inside his pants. Either way, big was relative. It meant different things to different people. And big wasn't always accompanied by talent.

"What do you say then?" he asked. "Should we go?"

"I'm fine here for a while."

He trailed a finger up my arm. "You won't regret it."

His patience apparently spent, he winked, stood, held out a hand. Under most circumstances, I would have considered the gesture a courteous one. Not this time. I rose and faced him, wrapping a hand around his belt buckle. I yanked him forward, pressing his body against mine.

He laughed. "Hey now, you … ahh … I mean, maybe we should save all this pent-up energy until we get to my place, sweetie."

I smirked, jammed a hand inside his pocket, fished out the wedding ring he'd concealed earlier. "What about your wife? Will she be joining in on the festivities too?"

His face paled, then warmed to a sharp, vibrant raspberry. "She's … it's … not what you think."

"It isn't? You're *not* married then?"

"No, I am. It's just … complicated."

"It always is with assholes like you, isn't it?"

He stroked my hair with his hand. I bristled.

"Come on now," he said. "Don't ruin our night together."

"I don't sleep with married men."

"You don't understand. Things haven't been the same between us lately. I'm not a bad guy. I just … feel distant. We're not close like we used to be. I don't know if I'm still committed."

It was a disgusting jumble of words from a man with no conscience, his eyes dead, without shine, like he'd strayed so far from the path he no longer knew how to find it.

"Married is married," I said. "Period. When you married your wife you vowed to be there for her for better or worse. Not for when it feels good. Rationalizing something you're unwilling to fight for shows me who you really are without even knowing you."

Aware the midnight rendezvous was now a fleeting opportunity, his tone changed from vivacious and flirty to stern. "Give me back the ring."

"Why, so you can shove it into your pocket and go for round two with someone else after I leave?"

"This isn't funny, Lacey."

"Good, Jordan, or whatever your name really is. It shouldn't be."

He swung for the ring and missed. I closed my hand around it and whipped it behind my head, tossing as far as it would go. Between the nineties rock music blaring in my ear, the crowd, and my increasingly blurred vision, it was hard to tell where it landed.

"You stupid bitch!" he seethed.

Instead of going after his ring, he directed his fury at me in the form of a balled-up fist. It connected with the edge of my jaw. A second later, as I fell to the ground, I caught a glimpse of Finch's fist as it struck Jordan's face, and he too went straight down.

CHAPTER 10

MY BODY WAS WEIGHTLESS AND NUMB, LIKE A GIANT cloud floating through air. I opened my eyes, staring at the mirrored panels surrounding the square box that contained me. An elevator perhaps. Finch cradled me in his arms, which made me feel stupid and weak.

He looked down, gave me a sarcastic grin, and said, "After I get you back to the room, I'll get some ice for your jaw."

I nodded. At least I thought I nodded. My head was pounding too hard to be sure. "You can put me down now. I'm fine."

Instead of complying with my request, he clutched me even tighter. "You might think you're fine, but you're not. A minute ago, you slapped my ass, said a few things I won't repeat."

No, I didn't. Did I?

I rubbed a hand over my face, winced at the pain. "My chin hurts."

"Do you remember what happened?"

"The guy I was talking to at the bar hit me, and then poof, you were there."

He laughed.

"You got a standing O from everyone in the bar when you stood back up. You remember that?"

I shook my head. I remembered landing on the floor, remembered Finch's fist smacking Jordan's face, Jordan going down. Everything else was a blur, except for a slight memory of me muttering something to Finch about him being the horse and me being the rider. The ass-slap assertion was starting to make sense.

I didn't need a rock to hide under.

I needed a crater.

"How did you … I mean, I know I told you I was going to the bar downstairs. I even assumed you'd follow me. But I didn't see you come in."

"That was the point."

"How long were you there?" I asked.

"The entire time."

"You never came over to talk to me. Why not?"

"I figured whatever's going on with you today, you wouldn't talk to me about it, even if I asked. And I'd rather you told me about whatever it is when you're sober. Besides, you did this same thing last year."

"Did what?"

His forehead wrinkled as he looked at me, like he knew I knew exactly what he meant. "Binge drinking."

"Drinking isn't a crime."

"I'd sure like to know what happened on this date that drives you to drink every year."

"Doesn't matter. The night's over now, isn't it? The clock resets. Three hundred sixty-five days to go."

"Drinking to escape the demons in your past won't change anything. Believe me. You'll never get over it that way."

I wasn't trying to get over it. I was trying to get through it. I wouldn't get over it no matter what I did. "She was so beautiful,

Finch. I can still see her face, you know? Every curve of her lips, every expression, every freckle."

"See whose face? Who's the *she* you're talking about?"

"Elena."

"Who's Elena?"

"She's ... I mean, she was ..."

What was I doing?

What was I saying?

"No one," I said. "She was no one. I'm drunk. I don't know what I'm saying anymore."

Finch inserted the hotel card into the slot, using his back to nudge the door open. He walked to the bed, reached down, yanked the comforter toward the end of the bed, and set me down like I was made of porcelain.

"You need, uhh, any help with your clothes and stuff?"

I shook my head. "I can manage."

I attempted to stand. Not a good idea. My legs wobbled like I was trying to balance my weight on a hoverboard, which was hard enough to do sober. I sat back down.

Finch glanced at me, shook his head. "Where are your night things?"

"My *night things*?"

He frowned, riffled through the dresser drawers. "It's not funny. Stop laughing."

"I'm not laughing."

He handed me a T-shirt and pair of cotton leggings. "Yes, you are."

I touched my lips. He was right. I was laughing. "I don't get it. I only had three, maybe four shots."

"Seven."

"What?"

"You had seven."

"Oh, wow. Seven. That's a record for me."

He turned. I lifted my shirt halfway, and the uncontrollable giggling started. "My shirt. It's ... well, it's stuck, Finch."

He didn't move, didn't look back. "Try harder. You'll get it."

Try harder.

It felt like I'd slipped the armhole over my head, and my fingers weren't coming to my aid either. Every time I tried to grab hold and tug the shirt down, I lost my grip. It was like my fingers were metal prongs, grappling at the stuffed cat I'd never win inside a toy machine.

"Finch, I need your help, and before you refuse again, you know how hard it is for me to ask for help when I need it."

He arched back, looking at me with one eye half open. "How did you ... what are you ... never mind."

He gripped the shirt, fixing it before sliding it over my head the right way.

I pulled off my jeans, flung them across the room, took the leggings he'd laid out for me and flung those too. It was too hot for pants. Much too hot.

He pulled the comforter over my chest, handed me a glass of water. I set the glass back on the bedside table without taking a sip, twisted his shirt, pulled him toward me. "You're handsome, Finch. You know it?"

He pried my fingers off his shirt, set my hand back in my lap, and went for the water again. "You really need to drink this, Joss. Then you need to get some sleep."

He walked over to a table in the corner of the room and sat down.

"What are you doing?" I asked. "You don't need to sit there. I'll drink the water. Go to bed. I'm fine."

"You're not fine."

"I don't want you watching over me. I'm not a child."

"You're acting like one."

He sounded mad, which made me mad. "Are you listening? I don't want you to be here. I'm the boss. You're the employee."

He crossed his arms in front of him. "I don't care what you want right now."

I wasn't sure if it was the alcohol, the emotions I'd been dealing with all day, Finch seeing me at my worst, or the fact I wasn't getting my way. The past twenty-four hours seeped in just enough to hit me hard. Embarrassed, I cocooned myself beneath the blanket.

"Joss, what's wrong? Are you crying?"

I felt the warmth of his body next to me, his hand on my shoulder. I felt like a fool. I was his boss. This wasn't right. "It's nothing. Please, Finch. I need to be alone right now. Okay?"

"I know I said you should wait until you're sober, but if you want to tell me what's going on, I'll listen."

"No, you were right. I should wait."

"Don't you trust me enough to tell me?"

"It's not about trust, Finch. Believe me."

The silhouette of the moon shone through the window, casting a ray of light across his face. I poked my head over the blanket just enough to see his expression, a mixture of confusion and hurt. "Don't be mad. Okay?"

He stood, tucking the comforter around me. "I'll leave you alone. Knock on my door if you need me. Goodnight, Joss."

CHAPTER 11

Elias Pratt
March 17, 1983
11:30 p.m.

OUT OF BREATH AND PANTING LIKE AN OVERWORKED hound, Elias Pratt leaned against the kitchen cabinets, sliding down until his backside connected with the firmness of the vinyl floor. He propped the pistol he was holding over one knee, muzzle still pointed at Donald and Dorothy Hamilton, who were slumped over on the ground. Dead. At least, he assumed they were dead. They weren't pleading for their lives anymore. Still, he wondered if he ought to plug them both one more time just to be sure.

For now, it could wait. The last several minutes had left him out of gas. Tired. He knew he needed to leave. He just needed a little breather first.

Elias hadn't expected the murders of Donald and Dorothy to take as long as they had, but then, he hadn't had time to plan it like he usually did. Hell, he hadn't even decided on whether he'd kill Donald only or the both of them until after he'd arrived, when fate made the choice for him.

"You shouldn't have gotten out of bed," Elias muttered in Dorothy's direction. "You might be alive right now. It's *your* fault you're dead, not mine."

It was a fact. Five more minutes to ransack the place, and her life may have been spared. She would have been out a husband and a few of her precious possessions, but she'd be alive.

Elias thought back to the events that took place in this room not thirty minutes ago. The kitchen light had flickered on. Elias turned just in time to see Donald, bat gripped in hand, shouting, "Stop right there!"

Elias had done what he was told. He stopped. Then he aimed and he fired. The first bullet went through and through, nicking Donald on the side of his chest before lodging into the wall behind him. By most standards, it was a decent shot, but in this particular situation, it was far from good enough for Elias. He needed Donald to be dead, and a decent shot wasn't dead enough.

Upon seeing the gun, Donald had dropped the bat and outstretched a hand in front of him, using his other hand to apply pressure to the bloody area surrounding his chest wound. Voice now soft and light, Donald seemed to understand his only option was to bargain for his life. "Now, now, son … let's talk about this. Please. If you could just put the gun down, you can take whatever you like and just be gone."

Put the gun down?

Elias laughed. Even now he couldn't believe the look in Donald's eye. The guy had really believed he had a fighting chance. The facts were simple. Elias's face was covered with a ski mask. He'd just shot the guy. It should have been obvious what was coming next.

"You deserve to die, and you're going to die," Elias had said before firing again. That time, the bullet hit its target, going right where it was intended. Donald went straight down. Elias stepped over Donald and said, "You're going to hell, sir. Right where you belong."

The commotion downstairs had awoken Dorothy. She ran into the kitchen, arms flailing in front of her. Elias steadied the gun. A single shot smack dab in the center of her forehead was all it took, and she too was dead.

Looking at Dorothy now, Elias couldn't peel his eyes away from the red ooze trailing down the length of her face. It slid down her cheek, pooling on the vinyl below. He wrinkled his nose, jerking his head in the opposite direction.

It wasn't the death itself that bothered him.

Death was a beautiful thing.

A peaceful, ethereal thing.

It was the blood that turned his stomach.

Over the past year, Elias had robbed a total of twenty-one houses. The first thirteen occurred without incident. Precious items were taken, but everyone lived. During his fourteenth robbery, the man who lived there caught Elias after he switched on the living room light. Without a ski mask to conceal his face, the old man recognized him, leaving Elias with no choice.

On the one hand, Elias had grown up a good Catholic boy. Committing murder wasn't how he was raised. On the other, something inside him had changed when he popped the old man. Something satisfying. Something he now realized had been there ever since he was a young boy.

An urge.

A festering.

A seed sprouting inside his young body, twisting and growing like the blood pumping through his veins.

He thought back to a fistfight he'd had with a classmate when he was seven. All the boy did was steal his money. Three quarters, one dime, and a nickel from inside Elias's desk. The boy had even left a note: *IOU ninety cents. Steve.* Steve hadn't touched his wad of dollar bills even though it was right next to the coins, in plain sight. Still, the rage Elias felt from his friend's betrayal wouldn't subside.

He couldn't leave it alone. He just couldn't. He found Steve in the lunchroom, grabbed him by his collar, and yanked him out of his seat. Once outside, he thrust Steve to the ground and jumped on top of him. He punched and punched and punched, until the principal wrapped his arms around Elias, tearing him off his classmate. Later that night, Elias's mom sat on the edge of his bed, her eyes red and puffy. She looked worried, but not just worried ... *scared*. "You're not like other boys, Elias," she'd said. "I guess I've known for a while now, ever since you stepped on our cat when you were three years old. I'm sure it's hard, but I need you to control your anger. Keep it inside you. Deep inside. It's important what happened today doesn't happen again. Understand?" Not wanting to disappoint his mother, he'd nodded, and from then on he pushed his feelings down inside him. Deep down.

Now an adult, everything changed when he'd murdered the old man. It was like a dormant switch inside him turned back on again. He developed a taste for death, an irresistible need that, in the last year, had only grown stronger. And now here he was, several murders later, having killed his first woman.

When he'd popped the old man four months earlier, it was an odd feeling at first. One part shock over what he'd done. One part thrill. One part wondering why he didn't feel any guilt after it happened. He'd stood over the man for several minutes, contemplating what in the hell must be wrong with him that he'd just committed murder, and yet he felt nothing. No sense of remorse, no sympathy—just a sea of calm. The festering wave inside him was gone. As a child he hadn't understood what his mother meant when she said he wasn't like the other boys. After killing the old man, he did.

Returning to the present, Elias clenched his hands into fists, pushing his knuckles onto the ground then boosting himself to a standing position. He walked over to the Hamiltons, gave each of them a few swift kicks. Neither moved. Satisfied they were dead, he grabbed his pillowcase of goodies and started for the back door, halting when he heard what he thought was the front door opening.

He glanced at the time on the cuckoo clock on the wall: half past midnight.

Shit. Shit. Shit.

It couldn't be. It just couldn't be.

Earlier that night at the high school football game, Elias had overheard the Hamilton's daughter Sandra saying she was staying the night at her friend Vicki's. This was why he'd changed his plans, decided to target the Hamiltons' house tonight instead of the Morrisons'.

Sandra wasn't supposed to be here.

So why was she?

The front door closed, and Elias heard the jangling of keys being dropped on a vinyl floor, followed by a female voice muttering, "Dammit!"

Elias's heart sank. He would know that voice anywhere. Sandra.

The distance between the front door and the kitchen was a short fifteen feet, maybe less, leaving him with little time to weigh his options. He should flee, hoping he'd be far enough away by the time she screamed. He had three bullets left, and he didn't want to use them. Not on Sandra.

The kitchen light came on, and Elias realized he'd contemplated his decision a few seconds too long. Sandra's ear-piercing scream penetrated the air, droning on and on until he couldn't listen any longer. He had to act. He had to act now.

The gun was raised once again, but Sandra didn't seem to notice it, or him. Delirious, she was only focused on one thing: the dead bodies in front of her.

Faced with the prospect of a shattered eardrum, Elias spoke up. "Shut your mouth, would ya? Screaming won't do anything."

Eyes wide, Sandra's mouth closed long enough for her to finally see she wasn't alone in the room. She took one look at the masked man in front of her and jumped back, stumbling over her mother's body in the process. She fell to the ground on top of her mother. Clothing now stained with her mother's blood, Sandra pressed both hands over her face and began sobbing.

Elias remained still, watching her. Frozen. Confused. Wondering why he wasn't running, why he was still standing there, unable to take his eyes off of her. He placed the gun on the counter, thought about walking toward her, but he didn't. "Please. Stop crying. Just stop it, okay?"

The flood of tears continued, followed by an eighteen-year-old Sandra muttering, "Mommy, Mommy, Mommy," like an inconsolable five-year-old child.

It was more than he could take.

"Sandra, please!" Elias insisted. "They're gone. They're dead. Get it?"

In an instant, Sandra switched gears, her tears slowing to a trickle. She wiped them away, glared at the man in the mask. "Do I … do we … know each other?"

He'd slipped, said her name. It was too late to take it back.

"We do, don't we? You *know* me."

Shit. Shit. Shit.

An awkward silence followed. It looked like she was thinking, processing, putting it all together.

Her eyes widened.

Recollection.

"Your voice … I … it's familiar," she said.

Even with the mask, it wouldn't be long now.

He thought about sparing her life.

Could he do it?

Was it possible?

Of course it wasn't.

What if she made the connection?

What if she figured out who he was?

What then?

He knew *what then.*

"I'm sorry, Sandra. I'm so sorry. This wasn't supposed to happen. *You* weren't supposed to be here. I never meant for you to see any of this. If I could just explain, you'd realize I was only trying to—"

He stopped. It didn't matter what he said now. It wouldn't change what had already happened.

A terrified Sandra squeezed her eyes shut and whispered, "You're going to kill me now too, aren't you?"

He didn't respond.

"Just do it." She buried her head over her mother's chest. "Get it over with. Do what you came to do. I don't care what happens to me now."

Sirens whined in the distance. They were coming. Coming for him. He wondered how it happened. Had a neighbor heard the shots and called the police?

Still unsure of his next move, he reached for his gun, shocked to find the counter empty, the gun no longer there. He turned his head, staring into the face of the person now holding the gun, aiming not at him, but at Sandra. Before he could do anything to stop what was about to happen next, a shot was fired. The bullet hit Sandra, slamming her body backward.

"What are you doing?" Elias yelled.

"It had to be done," the shooter replied. "Don't you see?" The shooter wiped the gun down and set it back on the counter, then turned and fled out the back door. Instead of sprinting to freedom like he'd done so many times before, Elias ran to Sandra and dropped to his knees. Pulling her to his chest, he cradled her. He should have been surprised at his actions, but he wasn't. The moment Sandra stepped foot inside the house tonight, somehow he knew it would all be over.

CHAPTER 12

Alexandra Weston
August 12, 1984
10:15 a.m.

ALEXANDRA WESTON SAT ON A STIFF, WOODEN BENCH on the fourth row of a Louisiana courthouse, listening to the grand jury indict twenty-two-year-old Elias Pratt on several charges of first-degree murder, followed by a swift, unemotional recommendation for the death penalty.

While the verdict was read, the majority of men and women lining the seats inside the packed courtroom smiled and nodded in agreement. A woman sitting in the next row fist-pumped the air. A man in the same row clasped his hands together and looked at the ceiling, like the gateway of heaven had been opened and his prayers had been answered. In another row, an elderly couple clutched each other, both gushing exuberant tears of joy.

Justice had been served for all.

Elias wouldn't receive a multiple life sentence; he'd be sent to Gruesome Gertie, the state's unforgiving electric chair.

Alexandra shifted her attention from the weeping elderly couple to Elias Pratt. He'd remained stiff and still while the verdict was read, like a pole rooted in cement. His hands were in his lap, fingers interlocked, his dull, blank eyes staring at the judge, as if she were nothing more than an extra in a lackluster movie.

He didn't seem to care whether he lived or died.

He didn't seem to care about anything.

It didn't surprise Alexandra.

Killers rarely did.

Dubbed the "Devil in Disguise" due to his boyish charm, middle-class upbringing, and devilishly handsome looks, most people speculated Elias was nothing more than a wolf in sheep's clothing, a sweet-faced rich kid disguised as Lucifer himself. Devoid of emotion. A psychopath. A serial killer.

Given his crimes, Alexandra could see why the public felt this way. As to her own feelings, the jury was out. She wasn't sure how she felt yet. Elias didn't exhibit the traits she'd come to expect in the David Berkowitzes and the John Wayne Gacys of the world. He was different. Not innocent, but different, with a quiet reverence that shocked her. Staring at him now, she realized in some ways she almost felt sorry for him. How crazy was that?

Court was adjourned, and Alexandra stood, watching the sea of onlookers who'd come to gawk one last time, to support each other with hugs, high-fives, and smiles of satisfaction. The judge called for order. No one seemed to mind him.

To most in attendance, they'd just witnessed what would eventually lead to Elias's end.

For Alexandra Weston, however, his end was just the beginning.

CHAPTER 13

Present Day

I WOKE TO THE SOUND OF ICE BEING JIGGLED INSIDE A glass, just inches from my face. I pulled the covers over me, refusing to open my eyes.

"Hey," Finch said. "It's almost eleven. You need to get up. You're meeting with Alexandra Weston's agent today. Remember?"

I groaned.

He peeled back the covers, pressed the cup to my cheek.

I swatted it away. "Come on, Finch. Knock it off. I'm tired."

"I'll stop when you get up."

He set the glass on the nightstand adjacent to the half-full glass of water from the night before. Then, in an extreme act of cruelty, he walked over to the window and yanked the curtains to the side. The room illuminated to a piercing degree, like if I looked at the window straight on, I'd see it was actually the doorway to the pearly gates. "You really hate me right now, don't you?"

"You have forty-five minutes to get dressed and meet Barbara Berry at the pastry place."

I flung the blanket off my body, realizing the only thing I had going on downstairs was a pair of black lace undies, and then I remembered tossing my pants after I'd refused to put them on.

Upon seeing me more naked than clothed, again, Finch jerked his head in the opposite direction.

"It's okay," I said. "It's just like seeing me in bikini bottoms, if you think about it."

"They're *not* bikini bottoms though. And they're see-through."

I looked down. Huh. He was right.

Without looking at me, he bent down, picked my leggings off the floor, and tossed them to me. I slipped them on and stood too fast, my throbbing head a quick reminder of the destruction I'd put myself through the night before. "I want to, ahh, thank you for coming to my aid last night. I mean, I'm sure I had it under control, but still, I took it too far."

He raised a brow. "You didn't have it under control."

"In any case, I'd like to just move past it. I shouldn't have let things get that out of hand in the first place."

When he didn't reply, I looked at him. He was eyeing me strangely.

"What is it?" I asked. "What did I say?"

"Nothing."

Saying "nothing" was his way of not asking me the same question I never answered when he'd first asked it. "I just had a few too many shots, that's all. You know me, Finch. I do this, what, once or twice a year? I'm in my thirties. I'm pretty sure it's okay to let loose once in awhile."

"You're not just letting loose though, are you? You're forgetting."

I socked him in the shoulder. "Oh, come on. Are you saying you've never had a few too many?"

He'd been avoiding eye contact with me since I got out of bed. At first I chocked it up to his discomfort about seeing me half naked. Now I wasn't so sure.

"Look, I'm sorry if it was hard on you to see me like that," I said. "It was unprofessional. I blurred the lines between employee and friend. I don't want you to stay mad at me."

"I'm not mad."

"What's eating you then?"

He wiped a hand across his face. "Last night, right before you fell asleep, you said something about a—"

He stopped midsentence, looked at the time.

"Something about a what?" I asked.

He shook his head. "You know what? It doesn't matter right now. We need to go. Never mind."

CHAPTER 14

I FOUND BARBARA BERRY SITTING AT A CORNER TABLE at Perfectly Pastry, nibbling on a half-eaten beignet, her eyes fixed on a cargo ship lazing along the ocean. Although her lips were coated in white powder, she was possibly the youngest sixty-eight-year-old woman I had ever seen. Her skin was milky and smooth; her sleek, platinum, shoulder-length hair was tucked behind her ears so no one would miss the gigantic diamond stud earrings declaring her obvious station in life.

I approached and she turned, aiming a pointy, ruby-colored fingernail in the direction of a chair next to her. She put the beignet on a plate, cupped a hand around a paper cup, took a sip, and said, "Well, this is a damned disaster, isn't it?"

I sat in the chair and wondered if the disaster she referred to had to do with her biggest moneymaker never publishing another book again.

"I'm sorry about Alexandra," I said. "You two have been friends for decades. I'm sure you're still in shock. I imagine everyone is."

She blotted her lips with a napkin. "No, no. I wasn't talking about how she died or the fact she's dead. I mean, Alex's death *was* tragic, to be sure. The disaster is the subpar coffee they're serving in this place." She frowned. "It's stale and bitter. We should have met each other at Café Beignet instead. They have the best … well, the best *everything*, but certainly the best beignets."

A waiter walked by. Barbara reached out, depositing the coffee cup onto a tray he was carrying, even though the tray was full of fresh coffee being delivered to other patrons. He flashed her a distasteful look. She flicked her wrist in return, like he was a meddlesome gnat she couldn't trouble herself with, and then she continued talking to me. "I just don't understand it. I mean, for this to happen now, when she was … you know … it baffles me."

All I knew was she'd just stopped herself from saying something she decided she didn't want to say. "I'd heard Alexandra planned to retire soon," I said. "I asked her about it, and she didn't admit it outright. She did say she didn't have the same passion she once did."

Barbara leaned back in her chair, crossing one arm over the other. "Retire? Alex? You must have heard her wrong. Scale back, perhaps. But retire? I don't believe it. She was devoted to her work. She would have gone to her grave writing." She paused for a moment then added, "In a way, I suppose she did, didn't she?"

I wondered if Barbara realized how heartless she sounded. Alexandra's death seemed to bother me far more than it bothered her, and I didn't even know her very well. I thought back to the night of the book signing, about the comment Alexandra had made. Was it possible she hadn't told her agent about her plans to stop writing?

"What was Alexandra working on before she died?"

Barbara's shoulders bobbed up and down. She didn't speak.

"You're her agent. Wouldn't she discuss it with you?"

Barbara shook her head. "Most of the time, Alex pitches an idea and we talk about it all beforehand. We'd have a brainstorming session, make sure the person she wants to write about is relevant, will sell well, has the potential of being a bestseller."

"Why was it different this time?"

"This time she knew what she wanted to write. She wasn't

interested in a discussion. We had a meeting set up for next week."

"Couldn't she have emailed the book to you so you could take a look at it?"

"Alex was paranoid about being hacked through email transmission and her books being read before they were released. Given the lengths she went to in order to secure her files, I didn't see how it was even a remote possibility. She'd saved the book to a flash drive for me, and we were to meet next week to look it over."

"And you were okay with not knowing anything more until the meeting?"

She raised a brow. "Do I look like a person who doesn't care about those kinds of things? At some point, I knew I just needed to trust her. Everything Alex publishes turns to gold, Miss Jax, no matter what it is. Believe me, I still tried to weasel it out of her, but it was to no avail. She simply said she knew I'd love it and talking about it would have to wait until we were in person. So here I am, and now she's dead."

"Do you think it's possible she'd already started writing a new book and that the subject of that book put her in danger or may have even been the reason she was murdered?"

"Anything's possible. She told me she had been working on the book for a long time. It was almost finished."

"Hmm. Who's relevant right now? Who would make a great story, move the most books?"

"You tell me. You're far more tuned in to criminal society than I am. Who are you writing about these days?"

Her evasive, non-committal attitude made me feel she was hiding something. Perhaps who Alexandra was writing about. I considered the most likely candidates. There was Harvey Lindon, a transient who murdered six women in Kentucky over a span of three months. There was also seventeen-year-old Steven Dent, who snuck out to the campground his parents were staying at, doused the tent in gasoline, lit it on fire, and burned them alive. Toby

Barker had an affinity for luring women he met online to his cabin, and they were never seen again. And last but not least, Darla Winehouse, a classy black-widow type who finally confessed to poisoning both of her ex-husbands in the eighties *after* she was diagnosed with terminal cancer a few years before.

"I'd write about Harvey Lindon, Steven Dent, Toby Barker, or Darla Winehouse."

Barbara shrugged. "I wouldn't waste your time on any of them. There's no motive. They're all behind bars."

My thoughts turned to Alexandra's current novel, *The Devil Wakes*. "Maybe I shouldn't be looking at the book she was in the process of writing, but instead should focus on the book she just released. What about Elias's family or the victims' survivors? It's possible Alexandra said something in her book that offended someone."

"Enough to kill her? Sounds like a lot of work to me. I read *The Devil Wakes* a few times. I didn't see any red flags."

"Well, someone wanted her dead," I said.

"Yes. Someone did. I have my suspicions."

"You have a suspect in mind?"

"Two. That's why I asked to see you today."

"Why me? I'm not investigating the case."

She laughed. "You're not, eh? That's not what I heard." She reached down, slipped a hand inside the front sleeve of her handbag, and pulled out a piece of plain white paper folded in half. She handed it to me. "I've jotted a couple of names down for you."

I unfolded the paper, glanced at the two names listed. Both men. Neither familiar. "Why didn't you give this to the police?"

"I did. I just came from there."

"And?"

"They listened to what I had to say with minimal interest. Who knows if they even took me seriously? I'm not waiting around to find out they didn't." She stabbed the tip of her nail onto the table repeatedly. "Something must be done. Something must be done now."

"This first name you listed, Doyle Eldridge. Who is he?"

"Alex's stalker."

My hand gripped the edge of the table so hard I thought I might snap the corner off. My breathing changed, staggered and rough. Restricted, like my throat was being squeezed closed.

I glanced across the crowded restaurant. Finch was still sitting alone in the same seat he'd been in since we arrived. Although he wasn't privy to the conversation I was having with Barbara, he cracked a slight smile, almost like he knew I needed it in that moment. Seeing him there calmed me. It also kept me from rubbing the three-inch scar on the inside of my right forearm until it was inflamed.

Barbara bent her head toward me. "You all right?"

I took a breath, forced my mind out of the past, forced myself not to think of the word *stalker*. "Fine. Sorry. It's just a bit warm in here today."

She laughed. "Warm? It's December, and I'd swear they have the air conditioning on. It's freezing in this place."

"Tell me about Doyle Eldridge."

"He's a squirrely fellow. Not much to look at. Good body for his age. Built like a linebacker. Been popping up at Alex's events for over ten years. Her 'most devoted fan,' she called him. She thought he was harmless."

"What makes you think he isn't?"

"He reminds me of the kind of guy who'd have a sick shrine devoted to Alex in his house."

She pulled out a cell phone, used her finger to type something, then turned the phone toward me. "This is Doyle."

She was right. He held a stack of Alexandra's books in his Facebook profile photo. His face was bent toward the stack, sniffing, like the books were a pile of sweet nectar. Good body, homely face. He didn't look like a killer. But then, killers didn't always look like killers.

"I see what you mean," I said.

She put the phone back in her pocket. "He showed up to one of her book signings a few years back with a scrapbook. The first few pages were filled with her book covers and articles about Alex he'd printed off the Internet. The last few pages were twisted. He'd clipped a bride and groom out of a magazine, replaced the heads with his and Alex's."

"What did Alexandra think about the scrapbook?"

"She laughed it off. They both did. He said he replaced the heads as a joke because he knew she'd like it. Seemed weird to me. Alex always said he was just a friend, that he'd been a friend of hers for years. I didn't believe it. A fan isn't a friend."

"Where does this guy live?"

"Are you ready for this? He used to live in Nevada. Then several years ago, he moved here. Said he was tired of the desert. Wanted a change."

"And you think he moved here to be closer to Alex?"

She turned her palm up. "In my opinion? Yes."

"I didn't see him at her book signing the other night," I said.

"What time were you there?"

I told her.

"Doyle is usually the first person to arrive, but never the last one to leave. He always struck me as the shy, introverted type. He arrived before the crowds, got his one-on-one time, then scampered away when the line started forming."

"You think someone as timid as Doyle is capable of killing Alexandra?"

"Miss Jax, even introverts have their limits, and quite frankly, with all the suppressed emotions they carry around, if you think about it, they're really the most volatile of them all."

I was an extrovert. I wouldn't know. But I did know a little something about the mind of a murderer, and she was right. "What reason would he have to kill a woman he had been so devoted to for all this time?"

"Jealousy. Read any tabloid over the last several years, chances are Alex and Porter's rocky relationship was mentioned from time to time."

Porter Wells.

The other name on Barbara's list.

"Porter Wells is Alexandra's husband?"

She nodded. "Weston was Alex's maiden name. Wells was her married name."

"Doyle obviously knew Alexandra was married though."

"When Doyle saw Alex, he'd say things like, 'Next time I see you, maybe you'll be single, and I'll finally get the chance to ask you out.' She'd laugh it off just like it was nothing more than a compliment, but I could see it in his eyes—part of him meant it. Part of him believed he'd have a chance with her someday."

"Did you tell her about your feelings?" I asked.

"I warned her to stop being so nice."

"And did she?"

"The last time they saw each other, several months ago, she was friendly like always, but Doyle was different."

"Why? What changed?"

"There was a nasty rumor going around alleging Alex was involved with another author."

"Was it true?"

"Yes and no. The two of them have been friends for years."

"When you say *involved*, do you mean—"

"Romantically, yes."

"Who is the other author?" I asked.

She blinked, didn't respond.

"Barbara, I need to know. Besides, if a rumor *was* going around, it's not going to make a difference if you tell me now, is it?"

"It's just … this particular individual, he has a wife. A lot of effort has gone into shooting down the rumors and making them go away. If you were to question him now—"

"If Alexandra was murdered in a jealous rage, the other man in her life could also be in danger. What happens if this other author shows up dead next, and *you* were the one person who could have stopped it?"

Barbara crossed one leg over the other, leaned forward, whispered, "All right, fine. It's Roland Sinclair. You didn't hear it from me. Understand?"

Roland Sinclair. One of the greatest thriller authors of our day. Married to actress Debbie Donnelly, America's sweetheart. No wonder the rumors had been squashed.

"You listed Porter Wells as a suspect in his wife's murder. Why? Was he jealous too?"

"*Jealous?* Heavens, no. In recent years, their relationship had become more of a convenient arrangement between two people than real love. And when I say convenient, I mean convenient for him, *not* for her. He sees other women on the side. Has for years."

"If jealousy isn't a motive, why do you consider him a suspect?"

"The divorce rumors were true. They'd been heading that way for years. For reasons unknown to me, she always hesitated to pull the plug though. Then a couple weeks ago, she told me she'd decided to do it. She even visited with her lawyer and started the paperwork, which was bad news for Porter."

"Why?"

"Alex had an ironclad prenup."

CHAPTER 15

ALEXANDRA WESTON'S HISTORIC GREEK-REVIVAL-STYLE home was located in the heart of New Orleans's garden district. The porch, which spanned the width of the two-story house, was accented by three symmetrically spaced white columns. The front lawn was small, but meticulously kept. I parked on the street, walked to the tall, iron gate out front, and attempted to push it forward. The gate didn't budge. I looked around, noticed a small metal box to my left with a red call button. I pressed it.

A long, sniffling sound emanated through the speaker. "Hello?"

It sounded like a female, but through all the wheezing, I couldn't be sure. "Hello. Is Mr. Wells home?"

"We're not accepting visitors."

"I was just hoping to—"

"Please. We just want to be left alone."

"Chelsea?" I asked.

"Yeah? Who are you?"

"My name is Joss Jax, and I—"

The gate parted, fanning out on both sides. The front door opened, and a young woman dressed in a simple black T-shirt, jacket, and black jeans came toward me. Her loose, long, caramel-colored hair was disheveled and looked like it hadn't been on the receiving end of a brush for a couple days.

I met her at the first porch step, noticed her eyes were puffy, swollen. She looked at me, then at Finch sitting in the passenger seat of the car, and said, "Who's he?"

"He works for me," I said.

"Huh. That's cool. I was going to drive over and meet you, but you'd already left."

"Are you doing okay?"

Her eyes darted to her bare feet. "I can't sleep. Can't eat. Can't hold any food down. My insides are all twisted and knotted up. I'm supposed to be getting married in five weeks. How can I do that now? How can I do *anything* without her here?"

"I'm sure your mom would have still wanted you to get married."

Her body wavered like she was too weak to stand up straight.

I wrapped a hand around her frail arm to steady her. "Why don't we sit down?"

She nodded. We sat on the porch.

A tear trailed down her pale cheek. "I'm supposed to be tasting wedding cakes today. Right now, actually. Isn't it crazy? One day I'm planning my wedding, the next my mother's funeral. Can you imagine?"

I could, actually.

Not the loss of a mother, but loss itself.

"You should concentrate on taking care of yourself right now. Your father can help with all the arrangements, can't he?"

"He's at the funeral home now. Why do you need to talk to him?"

"It's not a big deal. I can come back later."

She stared at me. "Or you could just tell me. The cops were here earlier. They questioned him for a while. Did he … I mean, are you here because you think he—"

"You're going through a lot. I'd rather not bother you with it."

"Why not? I *hate* him right now."

Under any other circumstances, I would have chalked it up to angst over her mother's death, but her teeth were clenched, jaw tight, eyes narrow.

"Why?"

"I hate him because he hated her."

"Your mother?"

She nodded. "He's not ..."

She let the words hang there, tucked her knees below her chin, wrapped her arms around them.

"He's not what?" I asked.

"Not the amazing person he wants everyone to believe he is. My mother was unhappy. She wanted a divorce."

"Do you know why?"

"She said he didn't love her anymore. He was seeing other women."

"And was he?"

"I don't know. That's just what she said."

"When did she tell you this?"

"A few weeks ago, right before she left for her book tour."

If Alexandra's life with Porter was so bad, why had she stayed for so long? For the money? The lifestyle she provided?

"If your mother knew about your father's other women, why didn't she divorce him sooner?"

"I dunno. I think she stayed for me. He was a crap husband, but he was a good dad."

"Did your mother say when she planned to divorce your father?"

She nodded. "As soon as my wedding was over."

I wondered if Chelsea had heard the rumors about her mother and Roland Sinclair. "Have you tried talking to your father about what your mother told you, just to hear his side of things?"

She shook her head. "I can't even look at him right now. It's too hard."

"I understand." I switched gears. "Did your mother say anything to you about a new book she was writing?"

"We don't really talk about her work stuff."

"I was told she was working on something new. She was just about to meet with her agent to discuss it."

"She wanted to retire, sell this place, move somewhere else and live a simple life. She was tired of writing."

I jotted my contact info down on a piece of paper and handed it to her. "I'll be in town for a few more days, maybe even more. I've written down the information for my hotel as well as my phone number if you need to call me for anything."

She slid the paper inside her pocket. "You're trying to find out what really happened to my mom, aren't you?"

I nodded.

"Why? Are you going to write a book about her?"

I shook my head. "I want to know what happened, just like everyone else. I've written a lot of books, interviewed my fair share of killers. You could say I have a knack for getting to the truth."

She leaned back. "Are you looking for my dad? If you think my dad would ever hurt my mom, he wouldn't. He's an asshole. Not a murderer."

Maybe she was right.

Maybe he wasn't a killer.

But it was possible he had the means to hire someone who was.

CHAPTER 16

I'D OPENED THE CAR DOOR AND WAS ABOUT TO DUCK inside when a flashy red number whipped into the driveway in front of Alexandra Weston's house. The coupe jerked to a stop. A giant of a man with salt-and-pepper hair stepped out. He was six foot five and every bit of solid. Dressed in a black leather jacket with the collar up, jeans, and square-toe, polished black shoes, it was obvious he liked to make a lasting impression.

He turned in my direction, lifted a pair of black shades off his face, and flashed me a sly grin that made me sick to my stomach, like he imagined me without any clothes on. Even with his chiseled Anderson Cooper looks, he radiated an uncomfortable vibe, and I found myself clearing my throat multiple times. Finch, on the other hand, was stepping out of the car and in front of me, like a hockey goalie protecting the net from a puck.

I stepped around Finch, attempted to walk over to Porter. He grasped me by the wrist.

I flashed him a look that said, *What are you doing?*

He leaned in close. "I don't like this guy."

"You don't even know him," I whispered.

"Neither do you."

"He's fine. I can handle this."

"I never said you couldn't."

He didn't have to say it. It was obvious.

Before I could say anything more, the man said, "Hello?"

I turned toward him. "Porter Wells?"

He held out a hand. I shook it. He did a quarter turn and offered the same hand to Finch. Finch nodded, didn't take it.

"Well, well, if it isn't the Nancy Drew of the Forensics Channel," Porter joked. "I imagine you're here to see Alex. Haven't you heard what happened?"

"I have. I was at the bookstore the night she died."

A second car turned into the driveway behind Porter's. Chelsea walked around to the passenger side and opened the door.

Porter looked at Chelsea. "Sweetie, can I talk to you for a minute before you leave?"

She ignored him, slid inside the car, and slammed the door.

Porter smiled like nothing had happened and said, "Excuse me a moment."

He walked to the driver's side of the car, knocked on the window. The window came partway down. Porter whispered something too quiet for me to hear. A male about the same age as Chelsea with short, black hair and olive skin smiled and said, "Sorry, Mr. Wells. Chelsea doesn't want to talk to you right now."

"Bradley, put the window up," Chelsea growled. "Let's go."

Porter grimaced. "Bradley, please tell my daughter to work on her manners and show some respect."

"Respect?" Chelsea spat. "You need to give it to receive it."

"Chelsea, if you would give me a few minutes. I need to talk to you about—"

"Stop it! Just don't. I want you out of mom's house by the end of the week."

"The house isn't just your mother's," Porter said.

"Correction," Chelsea fired back. "Mom's attorney just sent me a text. He wants to talk to me."

"About what?"

"He said the house isn't in your name. It's in hers, and she left it to me."

"What else did he say?"

"Nothing. Yet."

Chelsea leaned across Bradley's chest and put his window up. The car backed out of the driveway.

"Please, Chelsea," Porter pleaded. "Can't we talk about this?"

Chelsea pressed her middle finger to the glass, and the car sped up the road. Porter bowed his head, massaging his temples with his hand. "What a brat."

"Excuse me?" I asked.

"You saw what just happened," Porter said. "Can you blame me?"

"She just lost her mother."

"So, what, she gets a free pass to treat me like dirt? She's not the only one who's hurting."

He didn't appear to be hurting to me.

"Don't you think there's a reason she's acting this way?" I said.

"She's upset. Probably thinks if she hurts me, it will make her feel better." He raised a brow. "If you know Alex is dead, why are you here?"

"To ask you about your wife's life insurance policy."

Hands on hips, he tapped a foot on the ground like an unruly child. "Her life insurance? What right do you have showing up here and asking me personal questions that aren't your business?"

"I've heard a lot about you in the past twenty-four hours."

"From whom?"

"Doesn't matter."

"What have you heard?"

"You've had multiple affairs over the years. Your marriage was nothing more than a piece of paper you no longer honored. As soon as Chelsea married, Alexandra was filing for divorce. You signed a prenup when you married her. With the marriage over, you'd be broke, left with nothing. No money to pay for the lifestyle you'd become accustomed to living. Should I keep going?"

I expected him to blow up. Yell. Curse. He didn't. He shook his head. Disgusted. "You think I offed Alex to collect on her life insurance policy? Really?"

He snorted a laugh.

"I don't see why it's so funny to you."

"Oh, it's funny," he said. "Alexa isn't my wife anymore. She hasn't been for the last three months."

CHAPTER 17

PORTER'S REVELATION ABOUT THE DISSOLUTION OF HIS marriage was a bombshell I hadn't expected. "If you're not still married to Alexandra, why were the two of you keeping everyone in the dark?"

"I have my reasons," Porter replied. "So did she."

"I'm listening."

"For a long time our marriage had been a winding, nonstop, roller coaster ride, and I wanted off."

"From what I understand, the feeling was mutual," I said.

"I see how you look at me, like I'm nothing more than a money-hungry animal who cheats on his wife."

"Oh, so I have it all wrong then? You're a saint? Are you denying you were unfaithful in the marriage, trying to say you didn't sleep with other women? She's dead now. You can stop lying."

He shook his head. "Women like you are so full of prejudgments. You don't see anything except what you want to see, and you never will."

Finch cut in. "That's enough."

Porter laughed. "You think *I'm* the one keeping secrets? I confessed to mine. Alex took hers to the grave. And I have to say, she played the victim card for all it was worth. Even my daughter hates me."

"When Chelsea left just now, you tried to tell her something."

He nodded. "I wanted to be the one to break the news that her mother and I were no longer married. Now she gets to hear it from the attorney. Doesn't matter now, I suppose. Maybe he should be the one to tell her. She wouldn't believe it if it came from my lips."

It made no sense. A divorce no one knew about?

"Why would you agree to do what Alexandra wanted just because she asked? If you weren't getting anything out of the divorce, what was your motivation to keep quiet?"

He smiled, and my assumptions got the better of me again. There was only one possible motivation for guys like Porter. Money.

"She offered you cash to keep quiet, didn't she?"

He winked. "You're a bright girl."

"There's still something missing from this story though, something you're not saying."

"Perhaps."

"And now she's dead. What possible motivation would you have to continue to keep her secrets?"

"Look, Miss Jax. I'm not sure why you're here, or why you care about what happened to Alex, but you need to understand something. Despite how innocent she seemed, Alex made her share of enemies over the years."

"Enemies like who? Was someone threatening her?"

"Can't say for sure. My guess? She finally went too far, stumbled upon something she shouldn't have."

He knew more than he was letting on. I could almost taste it. Our conversation was a series of half-truths I'd have to sift through if I wanted to find the answers.

"Anything I say from now on will be to the police," he said, "and in the presence of my attorney. Goodbye, Miss Jax."

He turned and walked away toward the house. I felt defeated

and frustrated, like I'd stumbled upon something big, but I didn't know what yet.

Porter reached the front door and looked back. "Allow me to leave you one last piece of advice before you go. You owe nothing to Alex. She made no apologies to the people she hurt and betrayed over the years. Leave her murder up to the police to investigate, or you could wind up dead too."

CHAPTER 18

Elias Pratt
September 13, 1985

DURING THE TIME HE'D BEEN INCARCERATED, ELIAS didn't have many visitors. So when a young, thirty-something-year-old woman strolled through the door, ample hips swaying side to side, taut breasts on high alert like they were trying to bust out of her slim, fitted shirt, he was sure someone was messing with him, playing a sick joke to make his life even more torturous than it already was. The woman he'd imagined in his mind was a lot older, plain, and dull.

This couldn't be the woman he'd been told about.

Yet, here she was before him.

The woman flashed him a confident smile, flicked her long brown hair out of her eye, and sat down. "Hello, Mr. Pratt. My name is Alexandra Weston. Did they tell you I was coming?"

"Yeah," he said, eyes still glued to her chest. "They told me. You're some kind of reporter, right?"

"I'm some kind of writer. And … I'd appreciate it if you kept your eyes on me, please."

He grinned. "Oh, they *are* on you. Believe me."

Alexandra frowned. "Let me rephrase. Keep your eyes on mine. I can assure you, my tits have nothing to do with the reason why I'm here."

Balls *and* beauty.

She kept getting better and better.

"No offense, but if you wanted me to focus on your lovely face, maybe you should have worn a different shirt."

Alexandra glanced down, crossed her arms over her chest. Elias shifted his gaze to the woman's face, noticing her brow had started to perspire. Not a lot. Just a few clear beads of moisture. Just enough to make it obvious in an otherwise frigid room.

"You sure are pretty," he said. "Bet you get told that all the time though."

Alexandra gnawed on the inside of her cheek, tapped a bright-pink manicured fingernail on the table. "If you're not serious about talking to me today, Mr. Pratt, I can leave. There are other death-row inmates across the country willing to be the subject of my next book."

He leaned forward. "Chill, baby. I like the company. I mean, I'm glad you're here, glad you picked me. I'm flattered."

"I didn't *pick* you. My publisher did."

"I saw you at my trial last year. Didn't know why you showed up day after day. Figured you were with the press or something."

"I like to do my research."

"Fair enough."

"I'm here to write a story. *Your* story."

"A book?"

She nodded.

"You want to write a book … about me?"

She nodded again.

"Why?"

"Why what?" she asked.

"Why me?"

"You've become a household name. You know that, right?"

He shrugged. "Guess so. I don't know much about what everyone thinks anymore, now that I'm in here."

"People want to know more about you. About your life."

"They know about it already. Been in the paper for the last year and a half."

"It's not just your present predicament people are interested in, or the fact you refused to take the stand and tell your side of things in court. It's your past. What you were like as a child, as a teenager … people are curious. They find you unique and interesting. They want to know the person you were *before* you ended up here."

"Why does it matter now? I'm going to die. Why does anyone care?"

She crossed one leg over the other. "You're unique. You're attractive. Especially to all the women out there who see you as more than just a killer. They all want to know you. The real Elias Pratt."

"What does my childhood have to do with it?"

"Most murderers have a troubled past. They came from broken homes or suffered a form of serious trauma in their lives. You're different. You weren't raised poor. You had a good family, loving parents who had made a name for themselves in this town. What I'm saying is you don't fit the typical mold of a killer."

"So?"

"So, how does a man like you, living a life of privilege, decide one day he wants to aspire to be a thief and a murderer? What made you act on those urges, or were they even urges at all?"

He leaned back in the metal chair, grinned. "Those are good, solid questions."

"You've been locked up for well over a year now. Have you thought about it? Do you even know?"

He diverted his attention away from her, rubbing his thumb over a callous on his hand. He'd thought a little about what he'd done since he was arrested. Not a lot though. He didn't see the point. The pastor of his local church had visited a few times, always trying to elicit a feeling of regret from Elias, a feeling of remorse and repentance. The pastor went on and on about the importance of being cleansed of his sins by seeking out forgiveness from God. Elias didn't believe in God. He didn't really believe in anything.

Alexandra seemed to sense his thoughts had taken him out of their present conversation.

"I'm getting ahead of myself," she said. "I shouldn't have started by talking about people and their curiosities. I should have explained what I hope to achieve by telling your story."

"What you hope to achieve? It's all about money, isn't it? You can sit here all day and talk to me about how much you care about my story, about me as a person. Let's be honest. Your publisher only sees profit, and you only see publicity."

"I never pretended otherwise." She glanced at her watch. "I was hoping to achieve more today, but I'm almost out of time."

"I thought this was an interview. You just got here."

"This was only meant to be an introduction, Mr. Pratt. They don't give me a lot of time on these visits. I'll see what I can do to get a longer session next time."

Alexandra stood, her chair screeching along the floor as she pushed it beneath the table.

She turned, but he wasn't done with her yet. "I never agreed to a next time. I only agreed to a first time. Without my approval, you don't have much of a story, do you?"

"I'm not here to play games. I'll need to meet with you as much as I'm allowed until I have enough information for my story. Could be weeks. Could be months. Are you in or out?"

"Maybe I'm not interested in a book being written about me."

"Then why did you agree to our visit today?"

After spending almost every moment of every day wasting away in a cell without the stimulating conversation he craved, he'd grown bored. No one on the inside appeared to have an IQ over seventy, and for some, nearing *seventy* was even a stretch. Still, the thought of a book written about his life from someone else's perspective wasn't appealing. She'd write what she wanted to write, spinning his story any way she chose. Why agree? He knew how she saw him: Weak. Helpless. Malleable.

She was wrong.

Looking at her now, it was easy to determine her type—pushy and aggressive, a woman used to getting what she wanted when she wanted it. And even though he didn't know her yet, he didn't need to—he hated her already. And not just her: her kind. All the self-righteous women like her who'd looked down on him his entire life, even though they were all the same class of people.

No.

Even after all the effort she'd gone through to look irresistible to him, he wouldn't give her the satisfaction of being the patsy for her next story.

He opened his mouth, planning on telling her to get lost, but then stopped when another thought came to mind. In a game of wits, he was smarter. Of this he was certain.

What if *she* was made to be the fool instead of him?

"Mr. Pratt, did you hear me?" she asked. "If you weren't okay with me writing your story, why see me today?"

Voice somber and even, he said, "If I agree, what's in it for me?"

"What do you want?"

"Better food. A different cell. Privileges."

She tipped her head back, laughed. "I'm a writer, not a magician. You get to tell *your* truth. *Your* story. Are you saying you're not interested?"

He bowed his head, tried to muster up a tear or two. When they didn't come, he sniffled. "My family has been through enough because of me. I don't want them to suffer anymore. It isn't right."

By the look on her face, he could see his response wasn't what she'd expected. "Most people I write about want to be infamous, never forgotten. With this book, you won't be. Not in five years. Not in fifty."

"I'm not most men. I don't care about any of that."

"I didn't say you were. Look, Mr. Pratt, there's no set story here. If you're not the devil everyone has made you out to be, prove it. Now's your chance to tell your side of things."

"My side of things was told in court."

"Not by you. You pled not guilty, let your lawyers do the talking for you, refused to take the stand. You risk nothing by confessing whatever truths you need to confess now. You've been sentenced. Nothing will change your fate now."

"Nothing except my appeals."

She laughed again. "The appeals will only prolong your life for so long. In my opinion, there's no hope for a reversal."

"Don't say that."

"Ask me how many murderers on death row I've interviewed who survived. Go ahead, ask me."

She walked to the door, her heels echoing as they clacked along the surface of the floor.

"Hang on," he said. "How about a parting gift before you leave?"

Again, she turned, this time producing a smile. "What did you have in mind?"

"You can ask me a single question. Anything you like. I'll answer it."

It was like a rare diamond being dangled in front of a jewel thief, one he knew she couldn't resist.

She glanced at a silver watch dangling from her wrist. "We hardly have the time right now."

"Tick-tock, Miss Weston."

"Why did you do what you did?"

"Are you asking about the theft, the murders, or both?"

She met his gaze. "I'm asking about the rape."

The rape. He wasn't ready to talk about that yet. Wasn't prepared. He needed time. He kicked the chair back with his foot.

Stood. Said nothing. The guard walked over, gripping Elias by the arm, warning him to calm down.

"We're done here," he said to the guard.

"You said 'anything.' Not talking about the rape won't make it go away, Mr. Pratt," Alexandra said.

Without looking back, he said, "Get another patsy for your story. We're done here."

She gasped, then swore at him, the heels of her shoes clanking the way to the door.

He just laughed.

The game had begun.

CHAPTER 19

Alexandra Weston
One Hour Later

FOR A FIRST MEETING, IT HAD GONE SOME OF THE way Alexandra expected—a little push, a lot of shove, just like she'd done with every other subject in the past. She'd planted a seed, massaged Elias's ego with words to reel him in like "unique" and "interesting," attempting to make him feel different from other felons she'd written about in the past. It was the way her first meetings always started out—simple, unassuming, set up to give her new subject the idea that he was the one in control, not her.

A sprinkle of flattery, and the waiting was officially underway. She doubted he'd make it a week without asking to see her again, and when he did, she'd already selected another subtle yet provocative outfit for the occasion. The thought of him stumbling over his words to answer her questions was almost comical.

She'd feign interest, soak it all in, take notes, and pretend to be the kind of caring, understanding woman he'd always wished for in his life. Sooner or later, he'd have no resolve, and she'd have her next bestseller.

The theft.

The rape.

The murders.

He may have refused to tell his side of the story in court, but with the right prompting, she'd get him there, and when she did, he wouldn't have a secret left in the world.

Not once she was done with him.

CHAPTER 20

THE FOLLOWING MORNING MY PUBLICIST CALLED. BY the lackluster tone in her voice, I could tell she hadn't been successful in getting me what I wanted. "I tried to get Roland Sinclair's cell phone number for you," she said, "but I can't."

"What do you mean *can't*?" I asked. "Sure you can. Call his publicist."

"I did. He said Roland is very private. He doesn't give his personal information out to anyone."

"I'm not *anyone*. Did you tell him who I am?"

"I did."

"And they know *I'm* the one who's asking?"

"They know, Joss. I even left a message. They're supposed to give it to him."

"Mr. Sinclair lives in a small town in Colorado. If I can't get him on the phone, how am I supposed to talk to him about Alexandra Weston?"

"I may have found another way. I messaged him through his website and received a reply from his PA. She wouldn't give me her number, but she did tell me he isn't in town at the moment. I asked her if he knew about Alexandra Weston's death. She said he did."

"Did she say where he was going?"

"She only said the trip was unexpected. Last minute."

His sudden flight out gave me a glimmer of hope.

Alexandra's funeral was taking place in the next few hours.

CHAPTER 21

DETECTIVE MURPHY ENTERED HIS OFFICE. A MIDDLE-aged, redheaded woman followed behind. She looked tired and hungry, and though Finch and I stood three feet away, she never looked over. Murphy sat at his desk, looked at me, and said, "Thanks for coming in."

"You wanted to see me?" I asked.

He tipped his head toward the redhead. "Tell her what you told me."

I glanced at the redhead. "Who are you?"

"Celia Burke."

"Ah, you're the coroner. I'm Joss, and this is Finch."

"Yeah, I've seen your show." She had a sour look on her face when she said it. "Murphy told me you asked if Alexandra Weston was poisoned."

I nodded. She nodded too.

"She was. I found traces of fluoroacetate in her system."

Finch raised a brow. "Fluoro what?"

"It's a rodenticide," I said. "She must have ingested it when she drank the coffee. Did anyone test the mug?"

Murphy shook his head. "I didn't. It wasn't found at the scene."

"Wouldn't she have tasted it in the coffee?" Finch asked.

Celia shook her head. "Fluoroacetate is water soluble. It has no taste, no smell. It's not easy to come by anymore though. It was used on rodents in the '40s. Now it's mainly used against coyotes around here. They've been responsible for several pet deaths in the area lately."

"It makes sense," I said. "Alexandra was jittery, especially toward the end of our conversation. Her hands were shaking."

"The poison also caused her to vomit," Celia said, "which explains why we found what we did in the toilet. It's a nasty poison. The amount she consumed could have affected her perception."

"Meaning?" I asked.

"It could have made her hallucinate."

"Aside from the jittery hands, she communicated she was okay when I talked to her. What else did you find?"

"The usual … prints, hair fibers," Murphy said. "It's a public bathroom though, so there's a lot to go through."

"What about the knife recovered from the dumpster? Was the handle removed and tested?"

The question seemed to irritate her.

"The crime lab tested everything." She sighed. "The odds of finding blood were slim considering it wasn't the murder weapon."

"The killer must have been there when she died," I said. "She definitely didn't have a cut on her neck when I saw her."

Murphy nodded at Celia. "That will be all, Burke. Thanks for your time."

She walked out, leaving the door wide open.

"Is she always this happy?" I joked. "Is she related to Blunt?"

"She's on the shy side," Murphy replied. "She doesn't like people."

"I appreciate you including me, but couldn't you have given me this information over the phone?"

Murphy raised a finger. "I'm not done. Close the door."

Finch reached out, pushed the door closed.

"Porter Wells called me this morning," Murphy said. "He said you stopped by his house today, asked a lot of questions."

"And?"

"He didn't like it."

"Porter Wells called just to say he didn't like me showing up at his house?"

"He also asked for a restraining order. He doesn't want you around him or Chelsea."

"Are you kidding?"

He frowned. "There wasn't anything I could do. Of course, he can't get a restraining order over the phone. He needs to fill out a petition form."

"I know that and you know that, but he may not. Did you enlighten him?"

He shook his head. "I don't have time to hold his hand. He can figure it out like everyone else. I need to know why you went to his home though."

"Did Barbara Berry come talk to you yesterday?"

"For a few minutes. Why?"

"I met with her. She said she thought no one here took her seriously. She claimed Porter was after Alexandra's money and Doyle was a stalker."

"I'm well aware of her opinions. We did a complete search of Alexandra's home, talked to Porter, talked to Doyle Eldridge. There's no hard evidence on either one of them. Sure, Porter's full of himself and Doyle's a little odd, but you can't arrest someone for that. 'Odd' doesn't make Doyle a stalker or a killer, and 'pride' doesn't make Porter so money hungry he'd murder her for more of it."

"Do you have any other leads? Any other suspects?"

"Look, the real reason I asked you here, Miss Jax, was to remind you to let us do our job. I'm not trying to be rude, but maybe it's time for you to leave town."

I nodded and walked out of his office, leaving Murphy behind his desk, still talking to me like I cared what he had to say.

"Now hang on," Murphy called after me. "There's no need to get upset. I appreciate your interest and your help. And I loved meeting you in person."

I didn't turn back.

I didn't reply.

I just kept on walking.

CHAPTER 22

THE FEMALE CALLER ON THE OTHER END OF THE PHONE spoke in short, staggered sentences—fragments mumbled in strings of three or four words like the cell reception was cutting in and out. It took a minute before I recognized her voice. "Chelsea, I can't understand you. Slow down. I'm not sure what you're trying to say."

"There's someone behind me!"

"Who's behind you?"

"I don't know. A man … or maybe a woman. I can't tell."

"Where are you?"

"In my car."

"Yes, but where?" I asked.

She paused. "On the corner of … umm … Chestnut and Sixth."

Still in the parking lot in front of the police department, I snapped my fingers, got Finch's attention, put the call on speaker. "How do you know you're being followed?"

"Every turn I make, the car turns too."

"Can you tell what kind of car it is?"

"It's … ahh … dark blue, like a bluish-black."

"What about the make and model?"

"I'm not sure, an old lady car. It's big."

"Can you get a look at the person in your rearview mirror?"

"I see what looks like a coat with the hood pulled over the head, and he or she is wearing glasses."

"What kind of glasses?"

"Sunglasses."

"Hang on."

I glanced at Finch, weighing the decision I needed to make. I could get to my rental car and find Chelsea or sprint back to Murphy's office. I pivoted and ran, phone in my hand, Chelsea still on the line. Being a mediocre runner at best, I wasn't surprised when Finch shot past me. He flung the door open to Murphy's office. Murphy looked up and indicated we needed to wait. He was on the phone. I jerked the phone receiver out of his hand, slamming it down on its base.

He glared at me. "What in the hell do you think you're—"

Finch leaned toward Murphy, communicated what was going on. I grabbed a piece of paper from his desk. It looked important. I didn't care. I scribbled down Chelsea's location on a piece of paper, handed it to him.

"Chelsea, you still there?" I asked.

"Yeah."

"What's happening now?"

"Nothing."

"Are you still being followed?"

"Yes. I don't know what to do!"

"Keep doing what you're doing. Help is on the way."

"How far away are you? I don't know how much longer I can keep looping around."

"Stay as calm as you can. We're sending someone to you."

"My car is almost out of gas. I'm going to have to pull over."

In unison, Murphy, Finch, and I yelled, "No!"

"Don't pull over," I said. "Unless your car stops, you keep going.

Understand?"

"Yes."

"Are your doors locked?" I asked.

"Yes."

"Good."

Murphy leaned over to speak into the phone. "Chelsea, this is Detective Murphy."

"Where's Joss? I want to talk to Joss."

"I'm here," I said.

Murphy looked at Finch. "You two keep her talking. Have her circle the block a few more times until we can get to her. *Do not* let her park her vehicle for any reason or engage in any kind of contact with the person she believes is following her. Understand?"

Murphy bolted out of the door.

"Keep driving, but stay close to those cross streets," I said. "Detective Murphy is sending someone now. Can the person behind you tell you're on the phone?"

"I don't know. I'm talking to you on my Bluetooth through the car."

"When did you first notice you were being followed?"

"About ten minutes ago. I kept seeing the same car behind me when I stopped at each traffic light, so I turned into a neighborhood to see if the car would still follow me, and it did, through five streets and back out onto the main road I'm on now."

"Are you alone?"

It was an obvious question, but I asked anyway.

"Yeah, it's just me. I was heading to the funeral home. My mom's services are in two hours. I wanted to go early and, you know, spend some alone time with her before everyone else gets there."

Keeping her talking was keeping her calm. I kept going. "How was your visit with your mom's lawyer?"

"He told me ... he said ... my parents are already divorced. I just don't get it. How could she do that? How could she keep it from me? How could *he* keep it from me?"

"I don't know. Maybe your mother was trying to protect you." When she didn't say anything, I said, "Chelsea, you still there?"

"Hang on a sec. The car was behind me a few seconds ago, and now it's ... I don't see it anymore."

Murphy walked in.

"How far away are your guys?" I asked.

"One, two minutes tops," Murphy replied. "Chelsea, I have two officers en route. Get back to those two cross streets so they can find you."

A few seconds passed, and then Chelsea screamed.

CHAPTER 23

CHELSEA'S VOICE, PANICKED AND AFRAID, MEWLED through the phone like the wounded howl of a wolf—petrified, fighting to break free when there was nowhere to go. "The mother-effer is trying to force me off the road!"

A wave of guilt gripped me. I shouldn't be here in Murphy's office, waiting, incapable of helping her. I should have gone to her. Every agonizing second now was precious. Every second could save her life. It could also end it.

"Chelsea, what's happening?" I asked. "Talk to me."

"I have to pull over. I don't have a choice. I have to!"

"No!"

I faced Murphy. "Why aren't your guys there yet? How long does it take?!"

"They will be, anytime now," he said.

Eyes wide, he glared at me, no doubt a nonverbal cue meant to warn me not to increase Chelsea's anxiety level any more than necessary. I didn't care. I wasn't an optimist. I was a realist. "Any minute now might be too late."

The sound of glass shattering echoed through the phone. A car door opened and slammed shut.

"Chelsea, are you there?" I asked. "Are you okay? What's happening?"

"The car door behind me just opened. Someone's coming!" she screamed.

"Can you get away?"

Sirens whistled in the background.

"Get away from me!" she screamed. "I'm not going anywhere with you! Get away!"

A shot cracked through my phone's speaker, and the line went dead.

CHAPTER 24

THIRTY MINUTES LATER, I SAT ON A CHAIR INSIDE THE hospital room where Detective Murphy was having Chelsea checked out to ensure she hadn't sustained any injuries. The shot we'd heard earlier wasn't fired from an officer's gun. And it wasn't fired from her attacker. It was fired from Chelsea's mother's gun, which Chelsea had stashed inside the glove box after her mother's murder.

"I'm fine," Chelsea spat as the nurse inspected her. "I'm *not* missing my mother's funeral over this."

"Don't worry about that right now," I said.

"I'm not worried. I'm pissed that asshole got away."

The asshole she referred to had fled on foot after Blunt and Parks failed to catch him. Or her. We still weren't certain which gender we were dealing with. A tireless Officer Blunt was still searching. The attacker's car had been towed. Every inch was being inspected.

"When can I get out of here?" Chelsea asked. "Please. I can't miss the funeral."

"I have a few questions first," Murphy said. "Joss, can you give us a minute alone?"

Chelsea shook her head. "No way. She's staying. I don't know you."

Offended by the comment, Murphy huffed then crossed his arms. "You know I'm a detective. I showed you my badge."

"You ever see *Training Day*? *The Shield*? *The Place Beyond the Pines*? All cops. All corrupt. You seem nice. You're probably a great guy just trying to do his job. But right now, the only adult I trust besides my fiancé is Joss."

He laughed. "This isn't a movie. This is real life. But okay, if it makes you feel better, she can stay."

Chelsea glanced at the clock on the wall. "Can I be out of here in fifteen minutes?"

"We can postpone the funeral for a few hours if that's what you're worried about," he said. "After the car crashed into you, did you get a good look at the person following you?"

She shook her head. "I didn't get a look at her face, but I think she was a woman."

"What makes you say that?"

"She wasn't big, you know, like a guy. She was small."

Murphy frowned. "What was she wearing?"

"Black pants and, umm, black boots, the kind you wear in the snow. She had a black hoodie pulled over her head. It was tied around her face so I couldn't see anything."

"What color was the hoodie?"

"Black. Everything was black."

"Plain or patterned?"

"It was plain."

"Was there any lettering on the hoodie?"

"Nope."

"Any tattoos or markings?"

She shook her head. "I just told you, I couldn't see anything. She was covered up."

"Hair color?"

She rolled her eyes. "I didn't see her actual hair. It was covered by the hoodie. I *just* said that."

"How tall was she?"

"My height."

"Which is?"

"Five foot nine."

Murphy's cell phone rang. He answered, listened, then said, "Yeah. Yeah. Okay. Thanks. I need to put an APB out. Suspect is female, approximately five feet nine inches, dressed in all black. Hoodie, pants, snow boots." He gave some additional details and ended the call. "The car is registered to a Zack Montana. There's only one problem. Zack reported the car stolen a few hours ago. Besides the fact he's a guy and not a girl, he's also six foot four, so he doesn't fit the profile you just gave me. He said he ran into the coffee shop, came out, and his car was gone."

Murphy looked at Chelsea. "I'm going to let you go, but you won't be alone. One of my men will remain with you for now."

"Uhh, I don't want someone I don't know following me around. My fiancé is coming to pick me up. So, no thanks."

"Trust me," Murphy said. "No offense to your betrothed, but he can't offer you the protection we can. Besides, you don't have a choice."

CHAPTER 25

IT HAD BEEN SEVERAL YEARS SINCE I LAST ATTENDED A funeral, but in some ways, it felt recently familiar, like an ephemeral dream I'd had only yesterday. A dream that haunted my existence. It took every fiber of my being to remain seated. All I wanted to do was bolt out the back door.

Few things were certain. Alexandra's murder was personal. Louis's murder was personal, but in a different way. I still didn't know how yet, but they didn't feel the same. The failed abduction of Chelsea was tied to her mother's murder somehow. Although Barbara Berry had accused Alexandra's husband, I didn't believe he was the killer. He didn't care enough about whether Alexandra lived or died. Not even when it came to his precious money. He almost seemed relieved to be rid of her. I didn't believe he'd harm his daughter either.

At the back of the room, a man leaned against the wall, alone, his arms folded in front of him. He was too far away for me to get a good look at him, but for a split second he looked familiar, and I found myself struggling to draw breath.

"What is it?" Finch asked. "You okay?"

"It's nothing. I thought I saw … it's just … I thought—"

"Thought you saw whom?"

I was rubbing my wrist again.

Finch placed his hand over mine, stopping me from making my wrist any redder than it already was. He stood and turned, eyeballing the man until he was satisfied. Then he sat back down. "It's not him, Joss."

"I know. I know it's not. I can't help it sometimes, you know?"

"Nothing's going to happen. Not while I'm with you."

It was those rare moments when he wasn't that I worried about.

I shifted my attention, focusing on the people around me. Most of the funeral attendees were nobodies, people I didn't recognize. Scattered among them, attempting to look discreet, were a few officers dressed in plain clothes, including Blunt, who refused to look at me even though she knew I was there. Her eyes flicked around like darts trying to hit multiple targets, assessing every move, every twitch. My eyes were fixed on one person, Roland Sinclair, who kept his eyes on Alexandra's casket.

The services concluded with a song, and Roland stood. In his hand were two pink and white lilies. He walked to the casket, bent down, lifted Alexandra's hand to his lips, and kissed it. He tucked the flowers beside her waist, took a deep breath, then walked away. Porter approached him on his way out. The two exchanged terse words, none of which seemed pleasant.

Roland was the first to break away from the conversation. I stepped into the aisle before he passed me, wrapping my hand around his arm. "Mr. Sinclair, can I speak to you?"

Tears pooled inside his eyes as he looked at me. "Not here, Miss Jax. Come with me."

I followed him outside and came face to face with Doyle Eldridge. His hands were folded in front of his waist. He paced the area in front of the first step, scratching at his head, then brushed past me, entering the funeral home. I didn't know whether to talk to Roland or go after Doyle. I decided Doyle could wait. If he caused a stir inside, the cops would take care of him.

I looked at Roland. "Alexandra's husband just spoke to you. What did he say?"

"Porter Wells isn't Alexandra's husband. He's her ex-husband." A black Jaguar with tinted windows pulled next to the curb, stopping in front of us. He opened the door, turned toward me, and said, "Get in."

I surveyed the crowd still in the church and didn't see Finch. Thinking I'd be fine sitting in the pew for a few minutes while he went to the bathroom, he would probably be shocked when he returned and didn't find me inside the church. Actually, maybe he wouldn't be so shocked.

"I don't have much time," Roland pressed. "Are you coming or not?"

I slid onto the black leather in the backseat. Roland sat next to me. After the car pulled away, I looked out the back window and saw Finch, hands on hips, angry.

"Where are we going?" I asked.

"I'm going to the airport. Where you choose to go afterward is entirely up to you."

It was easy to see what Alexandra saw in Roland. Dressed in a fitted gray suit, he was sophisticated and tall, at least six foot four, with short, dark, wavy hair and tanned skin. He looked Italian or Sicilian and smelled of jasmine and bergamot. I hoped he didn't notice how I was shamelessly breathing him in.

"You didn't answer my question," I said.

"What question?"

"I asked you what Alexandra Weston's ex-husband said to you just now."

He twisted the top button on his shirt until it broke free, glanced out the window. "He blames me for Alex's death."

"Why would he blame you?"

"He has his reasons, which only make sense to him, I suppose."

What were his exact words?"

"He said, 'It's your fault she's dead. You murdered her.'"

CHAPTER 26

"WHY WOULD PORTER BLAME ALEXANDRA'S DEATH ON you?" I asked.

Roland tugged at his chin. "Mmm ... jealousy perhaps?"

"He knew about your affair, didn't he?"

"Alleged affair."

"It's been in the tabloids for some time."

He winked. "And that makes it true?"

"Are you denying it? I saw the way you looked when you leaned in to say goodbye. That wasn't friendship. That was love."

"Spoken like a true author. You have a sharp eye. Good for you. I love my wife, Miss Jax."

"And you loved Alexandra too."

"Would it be so wrong if I did? Most people are lucky to have one true love in a lifetime. I've had two. I don't regret it, and I'm not ashamed."

Forbidden love. It reminded me of the off-screen romance between screen actors Jeanette MacDonald and Nelson Eddy in the '30s, a controversy still disputed today.

"I'm not trying to pry into your relationship with Alexandra," I said.

"Then what *are* you trying to do?"

"Find her killer."

"Why? What's in it for you? You didn't even know her. Not really. Whatever obligation you think you have because you're here in town or because murder is what you write about for a living is unnecessary. The cops will sort it out."

"Maybe, but I'm here and I want to help."

He stared at me for some time before saying, "I'm not sure I believe you."

"That's okay. I'm not sure I believe you either."

He smiled. "What do you want from me?"

"Answers to my questions," I said. "Real answers."

"What are your questions?"

"In your opinion, is there a chance Porter could have killed Alexandra?"

"There's a chance any person you saw today did it, and though I dislike Porter immensely, it's doubtful he had anything to do with it."

"Why do you think that?" I asked.

"He's not clever enough to stage her murder himself."

"He could have hired someone."

"Again, I doubt it. Porter's not a trusting fellow. He's paranoid. He'd be too worried the person he hired would snitch, and then it would come back to haunt him one day."

"What about Doyle Eldridge? Did Alexandra ever talk to you about him?"

He nodded. "Doyle's a strange sort of fellow. You saw him today outside the funeral home, so you know what I'm talking about. I don't see him killing her either. He genuinely cared for Alex. I do believe he loved her and had felt that way for some time."

An oversized sign on the side of the road indicated we were within a few miles of the airport. I was running out of time. Did Roland have a theory about why Alexandra died? About who killed her? Would he tell me if he did? "Do you have any idea who killed Alexandra?"

"I have a lot of ideas. Doesn't mean any of them are right."

"Care to share them with me?"

"Perhaps. Not today though. I need time."

I wasn't the only one searching for answers. To whatever degree, he was too. The car rolled to a stop in front of the terminal.

"Time's up," he said.

I scrambled to find anything to say that would sway him. "Alexandra was supposed to be pitching an idea for a new book to her agent next week. I believe it was a book she'd already started writing, or maybe even had finished."

It worked. He removed his hand from the handle on the car door. "How do *you* know about what Alex was writing?"

"You first."

"Did Barb mention it to you?"

"Like I said, Mr. Sinclair. *You* first."

"Alex told me about the book."

"When?" I asked.

"Recently. Who told you?"

"Barbara. Was it going to be her last book? Was she really planning to retire?"

"Not just retire. Disappear."

"Why?"

"For all the notoriety she chased, she'd finally reached a point where all she wanted was to live in peace, away from the public eye."

"Her final book must have been important to her then."

"It was. She wanted to go out with a bang. I warned her against doing anything without considering the repercussions, but she's never been one to listen to what anyone else has to say."

"Repercussions? What was the book about?" I asked.

He raised a brow. "You don't know?"

I shook my head. He opened the car door, stepped out, and wrapped his hand around the handle of the luggage bag the chauffer placed next to him.

I slid across the seat, grabbing his arm for a second time today. "You know something. Something you're not telling me. What is it?"

"Sometimes it's better not to reveal things. Once Pandora's box is open, it's far too late. I, for one, am glad the book was never published. I hope it never will be."

He glanced at the entrance to the airport.

"Walking away won't stop me from figuring out the truth," I said.

"I asked you before why you're so interested in all of this. Why is it so important to you? And please, don't give me the same misguided answer you gave me fifteen minutes ago. Try again. Try the truth this time."

The truth.

This morning I'd asked myself the same question. I didn't know Alexandra. Didn't know her family. Wasn't invested in her life. And yet, here I was, involved in it like we were close friends.

"Well," he added. "I haven't got all day. Let's hear it. Hurry up."

It was hard to know which story to tell. The easier of the two would have to suffice. "A couple years ago, I lost a colleague of mine. No, not just a colleague. A friend. A woman who meant a great deal to me."

There it was. Raw, honest, real truth all sliced up in tiny, agonizing pieces.

He ducked his head back inside the car. "This woman. Who was she?"

"My assistant. Her name was Clara."

I'd piqued his interest. "How did she die?"

"She was killed."

"In what manner?"

"She was murdered."

He frowned. "Oh. I'm sorry."

"No, I am," I said. "Death strips life from us all eventually. I just wish it had come for me instead."

"You don't mean that."

"Most days I do. For five years, death has followed me like a boomerang, always returning, but never for me. People enter my life. Bad things happen. I survive. They don't."

"Why is your friend's death on you?"

"It's a long story. You'll miss your plane."

He let go of the suitcase, sat back inside the car. "Tell me."

"I'd just finished recording the opening segment of *Murderous Minds*, and the director called a late-night meeting. I sent Clara out for Chinese food. An hour went by, she didn't come back, then two. No Clara. I got worried, called the police. They said I should wait a bit longer, that she probably just got stuck in traffic. But I just had this terrible feeling, you know, a deep burning inside my body that kept growing."

"What did you do?"

"I borrowed one of the staffer's cars, took the same route she would have taken, found my car on the side of the road about six miles away."

"And your friend, was she in it?"

I shook my head. "The car was parked next to a sloped area that went down to the coast. When I didn't see her inside, I hopped the ledge and walked about halfway down, using my cell phone as a light. When I found her, she'd been raped, stabbed, and left like a discarded piece of litter."

He placed a firm hand on my shoulder. "You couldn't have known what would happen when you sent her on an errand that night. These things are unpredictable."

"You're right. There was no way to know what would happen. There was a way I could have prevented it though. Clara looked like me. From behind, she'd even been mistaken for me on several occasions. In the dark, in my car, it would have been hard for the man following her to know the difference."

"What are you trying to say—she was being stalked ... or, I

mean, you were being stalked, and the guy had actually intended to kill you instead?"

I raised the sleeve of my shirt a few inches, exposing the gash on my arm. "I had a stalker, and I was too embarrassed to tell anyone. Maybe if I had, he would have been caught, and she'd still be alive."

"That's quite a large scar. He did that to you?"

I nodded. "About halfway into the first season of the show, he started leaving notes on my car. They were simple at first. Legible. Neat. He said he watched every episode, was my biggest fan, that kind of thing."

"And then?"

"The notes took on a different tone. The writing changed. Instead of neat and legible, he wrote sharp words in all caps, said he dreamed about me, fantasized about us living together."

"How could you keep it to yourself and not tell anyone?"

"I figured it came with the business. I became more aware, kept my eyes open, carried mace in my purse, a knife in my glove box. I parked near the brightest light in the parking garage whenever I had a late night. For a month, the notes stopped. Then one night, I was carrying a bag of groceries to my car. He grabbed me from behind. I dropped the bag, tried to fight him off. He shoved me up against the car, kissed me so hard he bruised my lips. I shoved him off me, then saw he was carrying a knife. I raised my arms in front of me, trying to protect myself, and he cut me. I screamed. A man parked nearby came to my rescue, but my attacker got away."

"How do you know the man who killed Clara and the man who stalked you is one and the same?"

"He taped a note to the steering wheel. It said next time he was coming for me. The handwriting was analyzed. It matched the notes I'd received before."

"Did they ever catch the guy?"

I turned away, and he had his answer. "Every time I look at this scar, I'm reminded of what he did to me, what he did to Clara, the debt I need to pay. A debt I'll owe for the rest of my life."

The driver tapped Roland on the shoulder. "Sir, if you don't go soon, you *will* miss your plane."

Roland turned to me. "I was going to say my driver will take you anywhere you want to go, but your driver seems antsy to do the same."

"What drive—" I turned, subjecting myself to Finch's icy glare.

"Judging by the look on your—" Roland started, but I interrupted. "Bodyguard."

He nodded. "Okay, your *bodyguard's* face, you have some explaining to do. I'd venture to say you've learned from your mistake, Miss Jax. It would be a pity if something happened to you."

"How did you know he was here for me?"

"I'm a writer too. It's my job to notice my surroundings."

"Mr. Sinclair, I told you something private about my life, something intimate, something most people don't know about me."

"And I appreciate you for it."

"Before you go, can't you say something to help me find Alexandra's killer? Where should I look? Whom should I talk to?"

"Even if I gave you my opinion, you need to understand one thing about Alex. Her drive, her pushy nature to get the 'story inside the story' is what made her famous. That same drive created enemies when people confided in her and she betrayed their trust."

I was right back to where I started with him, listening to the same gibberish he'd already told me.

"Should I be focusing on the past or the present?"

"I don't know."

I didn't believe him. Even in death, it seemed he was protecting her.

I made one last attempt. "Who is the book about?"

"Talk to her agent, Miss Jax. But before you do, remember what I told you before. Some things in life should remain private. Some things the world doesn't need to know."

He placed his hand back on the handle of the suitcase, and I watched it roll away with him beside it. Our entire conversation wasted. As I slid out of the car, anger welled inside me.

Anger at Roland.

Anger at myself.

Anger for sharing something so intimate about myself and getting nothing in return.

CHAPTER 27

Elias Pratt
December 19, 1985
IT HAD BEEN THREE MONTHS SINCE ELIAS LAST SAW Alexandra Weston. She'd requested visitation several times, and each time, he'd refused. Agreeing to see her meant answering her questions, playing her game instead of forcing her to play his. In truth, he wanted to see her, wanted to look into her wicked, cat-like eyes, force her to see herself as he did. And he was lonely. Maybe even depressed. Visits from his family were scarce these days, and when they did happen, all his mother did was cry. His father didn't visit anymore. Almost everyone he knew treated him like he was already gone, even though he was still here, surviving.

Funny how life took so little time to change.

After three months of rejections, a desperate Alexandra had taken the time to pen him a letter. He expected it to be littered with pleas, begging him to give her another shot at telling his story. It wasn't. In fact, the letter wasn't a letter at all. It was a note. Short, simple, to the point. Her motives were clear. He had thirty days to accept a second meeting or her next book would be about serial killer Ted Bundy, a man she said was "the most famous and notorious serial killer of our time."

Ted Bundy.

Maybe he was more famous than Elias.

So what?

Famous wasn't everything.

Besides, according to the rumor mill, an author named Ann something, a close Bundy friend and former coworker, had released a book on Bundy five years earlier. Alexandra didn't strike him as a woman who would play second fiddle to another author who'd already published a similar book. The question now was this: Was he calling her bluff, or was she calling his?

For the next two weeks Elias read Alexandra's note again and again, unfolding it and refolding it until the paper had withered to almost nothing. He'd read it so many times it was ingrained in his mind—the words, the penmanship, the floral-and-spice perfumed smell of the paper. Alexandra's smell. He longed for her face, for the opportunity to get another whiff of her, and to break her before she broke him.

Alexandra walked toward Elias in the same way she had the first time they met, slow and sultry, grinning from ear to ear. The only difference was her attire, an unbuttoned jacket over a tight top and fitted, black trousers.

"Good to finally see you again, Mr. Pratt," she said when she sat down.

"Miss Weston."

"It's Mrs. now, but you can call me Alexandra if you like. How did it feel to receive a stay of execution last week?"

"Same as any other day, I suppose. I spend twenty-three hours a day in my cell. Most days I think I'd prefer to be dead."

"Do you? Prefer to be dead?"

"I'll die either way, Alexandra. All my lawyer is doing is postponing the inevitable. If you ask me, it's a waste of time."

She pulled out a white notebook, opened it, placed it on the table in front of her. For the next several minutes, he reminisced about his childhood. Occasionally she'd look up from jotting things down, smile, stare at him with those haunting eyes of hers that made him feel like she didn't just see *him*, but saw the darkness lining his soul too, thick and black like a corn maze at night.

After answering several mundane questions, she said, "Let's recap what I have so far. You were raised in a home with both of your parents and two brothers, no sisters. Your parents are well known in this city, both of them hard-working, loving people. You didn't endure abuse of any kind during your upbringing, not physical, verbal, or otherwise?"

"That's right."

"No childhood trauma either?"

"Nope."

"Interesting."

He shrugged. "I guess. Boring might be a better word. Or safe."

"Tell me about the first robbery. What made you do it?"

"I don't really know. I was bored, I guess."

"You *guess*? You robbed almost two dozen houses in a single year. What started it? Where did you get the idea?"

"The first house I robbed was done on a dare. My buddy James Hardy bet me a dollar I couldn't get in and out of his neighbor's house in less than ten minutes with a sack full of stolen items. I had to steal at least five things without getting caught to win the bet."

"Were you successful?"

"I was out in six," he said. "We had a laugh, and I figured even though it was a rush, it was all over."

"Why didn't you stop?"

"It was like an itch … you know, an addiction I needed to scratch. I started dreaming about it at night, plotting during the day, wanting to push myself to go bigger, better than before. I passed by houses on my way home and fantasized about what it would be like to rob the places."

"Are you saying you only did it for the rush? You didn't care about the stuff you took?"

"I'm saying once I started, I couldn't stop. I mean, maybe I could have. Who knows? I didn't want to. If I robbed a sixty-thousand-dollar house one week, I robbed an eighty-thousand-dollar house the next."

"Most of the items you stole were never recovered. Where did you stash the things you took?"

He leaned back in the chair. "Can't tell you that."

"Why not? The items are of no use to you now."

He grinned. "Next question."

"You shot and killed your first victim, Henry Collins, during your fourteenth robbery. Why kill him and not the others you robbed before him?"

"He woke up."

"Are you saying you wouldn't have shot him if he remained asleep?"

"Wouldn't have had a reason to, so probably not."

"You were wearing a mask though. He couldn't identify you. Why not just run, spare his life? He was in his late seventies. Too old to come after you, wasn't he?"

"For an old guy, Henry was a lot stronger than I thought he'd be. He attacked me, pulled the mask clean off my face. I went for my gun, a gun that belonged to my father. I'd taken it with me a few times before, but I never planned on using it. I didn't think I'd have to. I mean, I never thought I'd be able to ..."

"Pull the trigger."

He nodded.

"But you did."

Elias hung his head. "I'm not proud of it. It was an ... I mean to say, I didn't mean to do it. It just happened."

"What do you mean 'it just happened'?"

"I was holding the gun. He tried to grab it from me. I was trying to keep it away from him, and I must have squeezed the trigger. It went off. Shot him in the chest. Wasn't anything I could do about it at that point. He slid off me, pressing his hand to his chest like he could stop the blood from gushing out of it. But it was just everywhere."

It was a lie, of course. Henry had never tried to take the gun from him. He'd just stood there, several feet from Elias, eyes wide, shocked he was being robbed. The old man hadn't raised his voice, hadn't yelled, hadn't even tried to defend himself. The way Elias saw it, the old man was weak and tired, too tired to defend his own home. He didn't seem to care whether he lived or died, so Elias decided to help him out of his predicament. He aimed his gun and shot him.

The moment was euphoric and life changing, everything he'd hoped it would be. After robbing thirteen other homes, stealing wasn't fun like it was before. A part of him wanted more. A part of him begged for it. He didn't know why, and he didn't care. It was like he'd been freed from his box, and he wouldn't let anyone put him back in again.

The sound of Alexandra's voice released him from the memory. "Mr. Pratt, if the murder of Henry Collins was actually an accident, why didn't you admit it during your trial?"

"I knew I'd be convicted for all I've done either way," he said. "I didn't see the point."

Alexandra stared at Elias like she was trying to decide whether to believe him. He smirked. He'd done it—the wheels in her mind were turning, convincing her the man she thought he was wasn't who he was at all.

"I've never heard anyone say what you just said."

"Say what?"

"Take ownership like you just did. Most killers don't care about what they've done. They're proud of it. Even when they know they're going to die. I mean, some of them have a come-to-Jesus moment in the eleventh hour, but they're usually the desperate ones, those willing to do anything to be saved from execution. It's ironic, you know? For all the lives they took without hesitation, they're terrified of losing their own."

It was working. She'd separated him from the pack. Or so he thought.

"What are you thinking?" he asked.

"You killed a lot of people."

"I killed when I had to kill. Not out of a lust for it, and not because of a need I had to fill. I was faced with no other choice. I'm not like those other heartless animals. At least, I'd like to think I'm not."

"Why talk about it now? Why come clean with me?"

"Being in here, locked up, alone with my thoughts day after day, I've had a lot of time to think about those I've hurt. Family members of the people I killed who deserve answers to their questions, deserve to understand it wasn't personal. I'm hoping your book gives them the solace they need to move on. Closure, I guess. If it's possible."

Boo-hoo. That's right. Eat it up.

And she was too. He could tell by the look on her face.

"What about your other victims? After you killed Henry, you killed several more times. They can't all be blamed on people catching you in the act."

"Why not? You weren't there. You don't know."

"I suppose I still don't understand. Including Donald and Dorothy Hamilton, you shot and killed six people. You're saying all six posed a threat?"

"I'm saying they all had to die. I wouldn't have killed anyone if I didn't have to kill them. You believe me, don't you?"

"Why does it matter what I believe?"

He leaned forward for dramatic effect, stared right into her eyes until she stared back. "Because I care about what you think. I mean it. The only reason I killed those people was to survive. I knew I'd do prison time if I got caught. I know what you're thinking—I'm weak, a coward. I should have turned myself in. You're right. I should have."

He leaned back, watching her struggle to come up with the words that, up to now, had flowed from her tongue with ease.

"What ... what, ahh ... what about Donald and Dorothy Hamilton? The police found you on the ground, holding their daughter in your arms when they entered the house. Your mask was still on."

"All I can say is it was a different situation than the rest."

"Different how?"

"I can't talk about it."

"Why not? You've been open with me so far today." She paused. "Elias, how are Donald's and Dorothy's deaths different from the others?"

He shrugged. "They just are."

She leaned back in the chair, crossed one leg over the other. "I came here initially thinking you would be just like all the other criminals I've written about. But you're not like them. You're different, Elias. You don't say what you think I want to hear; you mean what you're saying. I can tell by the expression on your face. I see something in you I've never seen in the others."

"What's that?"

"Remorse."

He bit his lip, stifled the overwhelming urge to laugh.

"Yeah? You think so."

"You regret the murders you committed, don't you?"

"Of course I do. Every single day."

Bingo. He had her right where he wanted her.

"Help me understand this then. How does a man with genuine remorse rape a woman?"

When he didn't respond, she added, "I heard the sworn testimony given by Paula Page. I saw her tears, the way she couldn't look at you when she was talking. Want to know what else I noticed?"

Silence lingered between them for a time. When he didn't respond, she continued. "During Paula's testimony, she kept looking at Sandra Hamilton. I asked around. Paula and Sandra aren't friends. They've never been friends. Never hung out together. Why does a girl who has no affiliation to the other girl continually stare at her while she's on the stand?"

He shrugged. "How should I know?"

"After you killed Donald and Dorothy Hamilton, you shot Sandra. Instead of leaving, you stayed. Why? You must have known the police were coming. Why risk getting caught? What made her different from everyone else?"

"It didn't feel right, shooting her. I ... we ... knew each other."

"From school, I know. She said you don't really know each other well though."

"Not personally. I was a few years older."

"You shot her parents with precision, and yet you shot Sandra in an area you knew wouldn't kill her. There were also bullets still left in the chamber of your gun. Why not finish her off when you had the chance and make a run for it?"

He closed his eyes, shook his head slowly. "I knew this was a bad idea."

"You said you wanted to give people closure. Part of that closure comes from telling the truth."

He closed his eyes. "I can't do this anymore today. It's too much. I just don't want to talk about it anymore."

"Who are you protecting, Elias, and why?"

"No one. Nothing."

"It's hard admitting the truth, isn't it?"

"I don't know what you're talking about."

"I'm talking about Sandra Hamilton. You rushed to her side

after you shot her, cradled her in your arms, pressed your hand against her wound to stop the bleeding. Then you waited for the police to arrive, even though you knew what would happen when you got caught. Deny it all you want. I know why you did it, Elias."

"Oh yeah? Why's that?"

"You didn't just feel guilty because you shot her. You regretted shooting her because you cared for her."

"Who told you that?"

Alexandra leaned forward, curving her lips into a wicked grin. "It's a shame she didn't care about you in return. But then, how could she when you'd killed her parents?"

CHAPTER 28

Alexandra Weston
December 20, 1985

ALEXANDRA HAD GONE INTO HER VISIT WITH ELIAS Pratt expecting the interview to be no different from all the other interviews she'd had with criminals in the past. When it wasn't, it confused and titillated her at the same time.

Unchartered territory.

A killer who made her feel something she never had before.

A killer who seemed to actually give a damn.

A killer whose secrets she was determined to discover. If not from Elias's own mouth, she'd find another way. And she knew just where to begin. After being shot the night her parents died, Sandra Hamilton had recovered quickly. As an outpouring of love and attention flooded in from people who'd heard her story, she slid with ease into her newfound role of the grieving victim, weeping during interviews and even feigning a panic attack or two on air. She played the part well. So well, in fact, it was Sandra's label of Elias as a "Devil in Disguise" that took hold, sticking to him like gum beneath his feet.

One day after visiting Elias, Alexandra stood in front of the door to Sandra Hamilton's modest house. She knocked. No answer. She waited almost a full minute. Knocked again. This time, the door opened. Sandra poked her head out. Her hair was a matted disaster, her attire a short cotton nightie. This, coupled with the dark circles under her eyes, and it appeared she'd been sleeping all day.

"Who are you?" Sandra asked. "And what do you want?"

"My name is Alexandra Weston. I'm working on a book about Elias Pratt."

"So?"

"Can I come in?"

"No."

"I tried calling several times yesterday. I even left messages on your answering machine. You never called me back."

Sandra moved a hand to her hip. "What do you think that means?"

"You don't want to talk to me."

"Good. You're smarter than you look."

Sandra turned and walked away, leaving the door ajar. Alexandra took it as a sign she'd been offered a full-access pass and stepped inside. Sandra stopped at the kitchen, reached for a pack of cigarettes on the counter. She cupped a hand around her lips, lit up, took a long drag, and blew smoke into the air, allowing the smell of tobacco to waft through the room.

From the back of a long hallway, a man emerged from a bedroom. He was dressed in nothing but a pair of boxer shorts and looked like he exceeded Sandra's age by at least fifteen years. He scratched at his family jewels, gave Alexandra a quick head nod, smiled, and continued to scratch away until he, too, reached the kitchen.

He looked at Sandra. "Who's your friend?"

Sandra whipped around, glared at Alexandra. "You need to go. I don't have time for this."

"I need to ask you a few questions."

Sandra glanced at a clock on the wall, tensed. "You have to go, Ben. Now."

"Already?" he asked. "Feels like I just got here, baby. Can I see you again?"

"Maybe. I'll call you."

"What about tomorrow? I can come over after work. Five thirty be okay?"

"I said I'd call you."

The man hung his head, returned to the bedroom. Alexandra assumed, and hoped, it was to get his clothes and be on his way. Seconds later, the doorbell rang.

A different man, this time a bit closer to Sandra in age, entered the house. "It's Roger," he hollered into the house. "The door's open. I'm coming in."

Sandra flicked the cigarette into an ashtray and marched over to him. "You're early, Roger. Fifteen minutes early. We talked about this. I give you a time. You stick to it, or there won't be a next time. Understand?"

Roger produced a handful of red roses, offered them to Sandra. She smacked them away. "No, no, no. Roger. I told you. It isn't like that. Now leave."

"But what about—"

"Come back in fifteen minutes."

Sandra slammed the door, yelled, "Ben, I told you to get out!"

"I'm coming, I'm coming," he yelled back.

He shuffled down the hall, leaned toward Sandra on his way out like he wanted to give her a kiss. She jerked her face in the opposite direction, and his kiss landed on her hair.

Once he'd left, Alexandra said, "What the hell is going on here? Why are men coming in and out of your house today?"

Sandra shrugged. "Don't worry about it. It's nothing."

"Doesn't look like nothing."

"Does it *look like* your business? Because it isn't."

"I have a few questions about Elias," Alexandra said. "Answer them and I'll leave you to get back to whatever the 'nothing' is you have going here."

"I'm not interested in talking about Elias. It's been almost three years. I don't think about it anymore. Are we done?"

"Are you aware Elias was just granted another stay of execution?"

"Do you think I care? Do I *look like* I care? I don't keep up on any of it anymore. Not since the trial ended."

"Your parents are dead because of him. That doesn't matter to you?"

"He got what he deserved. I've moved on. Everyone else should too."

"I'm glad to hear it. Still, must have been hard after what he did to you."

Sandra turned, coughed. "What he did … it doesn't … I'm not … I'm fine."

"I talked to your neighbor."

"So?"

"The one who called the police the night Elias broke in. She saw you come home that night. Knew the exact time too."

"Your point?"

"When she heard the gunshot, the one after you arrived home, the one that hit you, it was at least ten minutes before police arrived. A lot of time, isn't it?"

"I'm not sure what you mean."

"You do though, don't you, Sandra? You know exactly what I mean. He could have left if he wanted to. He didn't. He stayed. And the only reason I can think of is that he stayed for you."

Sandra shrugged. "So."

"The first officer on the scene said that when he walked into the house Elias was cradling you, saying, 'It's all right. Everything's going to be all right now. I'm not going to leave you.' Interesting choice of words, don't you think?"

"The guy's a freaking weirdo. Why does it matter what he said?"

"When Paula Page was on the stand during Elias's trial, she kept looking at you. Do you have any idea why?"

"I don't know her. Who knows?" Sandra pointed to the door. "You need to leave."

Alexandra walked to the door, turning back before she stepped outside. "There's a reason Elias saved you. I think you know why, and I won't stop digging until I figure it all out."

Sandra curved her lips into a wry grin and leaned forward. "Good luck. You'll need it."

CHAPTER 29

Alexandra Weston
March 3, 1985
5:30 p.m.

IF ALEXANDRA COULDN'T GET SANDRA HAMILTON TO talk, she knew the perfect alternative: Paula Page. Aside from the fact both women went to the same school and were the same age during Elias's crime spree, Paula was Sandra's opposite in every way. Reticent. Shy. The kind of girl no one noticed in school because, most of the time, no one knew she was there. She was a lurker, always in the shadows, watching from the sidelines, not one to engage.

Less than a year after she graduated, Paula married James Keller, a pastor seven years her senior whom she'd only dated for three months. Staring at the two of them now, sitting a foot apart from each another on the couch, Alexandra couldn't imagine a more boring, mundane couple.

While James appeared confident in his cheap church suit and paisley tie, a dirty-blond, curly-haired Paula, in a simple, understated dress, acted anxious and uncomfortable. Hands pressed together between her legs, her breathing was abnormal, heavy, like she knew what was coming.

"You say you're writing a book about Elias Pratt?" James asked.

"I am," Alexandra responded. "And I was hoping to speak with Paula alone."

"You think I'm going to leave you alone with my wife?"

"I was hoping for a few minutes with her on my own, yes."

He laughed. "We're a team. What we do, we do together. The only way I'll allow you to talk to her at all is if I'm present. I also want to look over and approve anything you want to put in the book you're writing, pertaining to my wife. Deal?"

Alexandra smiled the way she always did in these situations. A smile she'd perfected. A smile that said *Trust me, everything's going to be okay.* Her artificial smile was accompanied by the perfect tone of voice. Low. Pleasant. Reassuring. "Of course, Mr. Keller. I completely understand. How lucky Paula is to have a caring husband like you! Truly. She's a lucky woman."

Before that moment, James's back had been arched, his head held forward and high, like an eagle protecting his nest. Now he leaned back, crossed one leg over the other. Smiled. "Thank you. You're very observant. I can see how you would be in your line of work."

No, thank YOU, Alexandra thought.

"The women who read my book will be inspired by your story, Paula."

Her cheeks turned bright pink in color. "You really think so?"

"I do." Alexandra switched gears. "I'd like to go over the statement you gave to the police, Paula, and what you said on the stand during Elias's trial."

"Why? I said everything I needed to say back then. You can take my statement and use that in your book, right?"

"I could. It's not the same thing though. Talking to you in person allows me to get a sense of what you endured on a personal level so I can accurately express it to my readers. I want everyone to see Elias as the sinner he is, and you as the innocent victim."

James's profuse nod of agreement was the approval Paula needed to respond.

"I don't remember much about it anymore," she said. "I've blocked it out. I try not to think about that night."

What an interesting statement, and oddly similar to the one Sandra had given.

"I'm sure it's hard to talk about, even now. I'll be brief, okay?"

"It's just, you're asking me to live through it all again. I don't think I want to—"

James grabbed Paula's hand. "Be brave, honey. Think about what she said. Think about the lives you'll touch with your story, the women out there suffering through the same thing you suffered through. Look at where you are now. You'll give them hope."

She nodded like the lifeless, subservient housewife Alexandra saw her to be.

James looked at Alexandra. "Ask your questions."

"I want to talk about the timeline of the night Elias broke into your parents' house. Can you take me through it?"

"All of it?" Paula asked.

Alexandra nodded. "Just once. Once is all I need, and then I have just a few more questions, and we'll be done. Sound good?"

"I was asleep in bed," Paula said. "I, umm, heard a noise downstairs. At first I thought it was my parents. I looked at my watch. It was almost two in the morning, and they never stayed up later than ten."

"Then what happened?"

"I thought if it wasn't my parents, it might be Amanda, and maybe the noise was coming from outside, not inside."

"Who's Amanda?"

"My next-door neighbor at the time. Sometimes she snuck out late at night to see the guy she was dating. If the door to her house was locked when she got back home, she'd climb the tree in between our two houses and go through her bedroom window. I thought maybe she was outside talking to her boyfriend, but when I looked outside, no one was there."

"You told police you were assaulted in your room."

Paula nodded, her arms and hands trembling. "I was looking out the window and Elias grabbed me from behind."

"How can you be sure it was Elias who grabbed you?"

"When he was arrested, the news showed photos of the mask. It was the same one I saw the night he was in our house."

"Did Elias say anything to you when he grabbed you?"

"He put his hand over my mouth, a knife to my neck, and told me not to say a word."

"Which hand was the knife in?"

She tilted her head, thinking. "The left."

"Are you sure?"

"Yes."

"He wasn't left-handed though, he was right-handed. And you said the knife was in his right hand when you were questioned as well." Alexandra pulled a piece of paper from a folder in her briefcase. "I know it's been a while. Would you like to look over what you originally told police?"

"I *know* what I said."

Clearly, she didn't. Alexandra also found it curious Paula said Elias had a knife when he'd only been known to carry a gun.

"I didn't mean to upset you." Alexandra said. "Go on. What happened next?"

Elias pushed me down on the bed, got on top of me. And then he … then he …"

"I'm sure you don't need her to recall what transpired next," James said. "We all know what happened."

"Paula," Alexandra said. "I spoke to Sandra today, right before I came here. She had some interesting things to say. Do you know her?"

Paula's reddened face paled, the color draining from her skin like fabric baked by the sun for too long. "I don't know Sandra. Not personally."

"She's been visiting Elias in prison. Did you know that?"

It was a lie of course. One Alexandra hoped she'd spun in her favor. From the unpleasant expression on Paula's face, it was working. Now for the big finish.

"I was also inside the courtroom the day you took the stand against Elias," Alexandra said. "You kept looking over at Sandra while you gave your testimony. Can you tell me why?"

"I don't know. I don't remember looking at her at all."

"But you did. Several times."

Before James had the chance to step in, Alexandra stood. "I can see talking about Elias is still too hard for you, Paula, and I have an appointment with Detective Murphy, so I need to go."

This was also a lie, of course, to gauge Paula's reaction. And it worked.

Paula's eyes widened. "Why are you seeing him? To interview him for your book?"

"A few things have come to light since I started my book," Alexandra said. "Things I feel Detective Murphy deserves to know. Are you sure there isn't anything else you want to tell me before I go?"

"What are you suggesting?" James asked. "You're acting like my wife has something to hide. She doesn't. Whatever Elias Pratt is filling Sandra Hamilton's head with, I'm sure it's nothing but a pile of lies."

"I'm sure you're right. Still, it's my duty to share things with the police from time to time, especially things relevant to a case like this one."

James turned to Paula. "There isn't anything Elias could say that has anything to do with you. Right, honey?"

Paula shielded her face with her hands, tears spilling out from the corners.

"What are you doing?" he asked. "You have nothing to hide. Nothing to be ashamed of. Why are you crying?"

"I don't know. I ..."

He clasped his hands over hers. "Paula, you don't have to talk about this anymore, or ever again as far as I'm concerned. You're free of all this now. It's in the past."

"It's not," Paula sobbed.

"Of course it is."

"No, I mean, it really isn't, James."

"I don't understand. Why not?"

"Because I know what Elias told her, and it's true. Elias never raped me, and—"

Alexandra pointed a finger. "I *knew* it! I knew you were hiding something."

"Wait," Paula said. "Are you saying you didn't already know about what I just said?"

"That's exactly what I'm saying."

"But you said you were going to see Detective Murphy. You said Sandra and Elias had spoken."

Alexandra raised both hands in the air. "Did I? It's called lying, honey. And now you understand why I did it. You and Sandra must have had an agreement of some kind, although I still don't know how she roped you in or why she chose you."

Eyes wide, Paula turned toward her husband. "James, I'm sorry. It was a mistake, an accident. I'm a different person now."

James raised a hand, and Paula went silent. "Don't say another word, Paula. And Mrs. Weston, it's time for you to leave."

CHAPTER 30

Elias Pratt
January 13, 1986

ELIAS WATCHED AS ALEXANDRA PRANCED INTO THE room, like she was having the best day of her life. She plopped onto the seat across from him, causing the button holding together her rayon suit jacket to spread open, giving Elias a visual of her blush-colored lingerie underneath and, along with it, a sizeable helping of cleavage. Alexandra glanced down, realizing the mishap, and grinned, this time seeming to welcome the attention and doing nothing to stop it.

"I have news," she said. "And it's taken me three weeks to get authorization to see you again, or I would have told you sooner."

"What kind of news?" Elias asked.

"The best kind. After I spoke to you last, I went to see Sandra Hamilton."

"Why?"

"I wanted to question her about the night you killed her parents."

He grimaced, irritated by her careless attitude. "I don't understand why you wanted to talk to Sandra. I'm giving you the story you want, *and* I'm giving you everything you need. Leave her out of it."

Alexandra smiled. "If you were giving me everything I need, I wouldn't have talked to her. You're not though, Elias, and you haven't been. A piece of your story involves Sandra. A very big piece, considering you are where you are right now because of her. Besides, it's too late now."

Listening to Alexandra flaunt her power and his helplessness sickened him, rustling the burning fire from within. She could do whatever she liked, and she wanted him to know it. There was nothing he could do to stop her. Even if he refused to speak, the book would go on with or without him. If only there was something he could do to even the score, to make her lose the upper hand she had over him.

If only.

"How is Sandra?" he asked.

"Loose."

"Meaning?"

"There were half-naked guys coming in and out of her place like she was running a one-woman brothel, which I assume is exactly what she has going on."

He shook his head.

No.

It couldn't be true.

He didn't believe it.

Alexandra was lying.

She had to be.

"I don't believe you," he said. "Sandra's not that kind of girl. You must be mistaken."

"I was there. I know what I saw."

"What were their names?"

"Whose names?"

"The names of the men at her house," he said.

She told him.

"Describe them to me," he said. "What did they look like?"

"Why does it matter so much to you, Elias?"

"Because I asked."

She complied, but it didn't matter. He didn't know either of the men. "What did you say to Sandra?"

"I told her who I was and what I wanted. She wasn't interested in talking. She asked me to leave, and I did."

"That's it?" he said. "That's your news?"

She shook her head. "After I left Sandra's house, I went to see Paula Page. You'll never guess what *she* told me."

Except he could guess. The only question now was what all she'd divulged.

Alexandra cocked her head to the side. "Paula told me she wasn't raped the night you broke into her parents' house. Why would she perjure herself in court?"

He shrugged. Alexandra continued.

"She aligned herself with Sandra Hamilton, and although it doesn't make sense to me why Paula allowed herself to be manipulated, or why Sandra wanted her to say she was raped in the first place, Paula still did Sandra's bidding."

"You don't know if anything you're saying is true. You're just guessing."

"Paula's a religious woman now. A preacher's wife." Alexandra laughed. "Maybe the fear of God got into her after what she did, and so she decided marrying a servant of God might make up for it."

Elias knew what had gotten into Paula. The woman sitting right in front of him.

"I know what you're thinking," Alexandra said, "but she should have thought of the consequences before she lied. And while we're on the subject, why did she do it? Why lie in the first place? And why would you take responsibility for it?"

"I *didn't* take responsibility for it."

"You confessed."

"To the murders, not the rape."

"You didn't dispute the rape in court. You may as well have taken responsibility. You do understand that, right? By refusing to talk, you look guilty."

"If you reveal what Paula did, she could face jail time. Or do you even care?"

"I'd be lying if I said my book doesn't matter to me. I care about every book I write. You may be a murderer, but you were wrongly accused of a rape you didn't commit. The public deserves to know. And they will."

"You'll ruin her," Elias said. "People will never look at her in the same way."

Alexandra leaned back in the chair, studied Elias's face for a moment. "I don't understand. Why would you defend Paula? What reason would you possibly have for protecting her right now?"

"My fate was sealed with the murders. Coming out against Paula may add a dash of spice to the story, but it won't change anything. Just … think about it before you ruin her life for no reason."

Alexandra crossed one leg over the other, looked at Elias the same way she had during their last visit, when she thought she saw the humanity in him. "You surprise me every time I'm here, Elias."

"Why, because you think I'm a decent human being? I'm not."

She leaned forward. "See, I didn't think so at first, but you are. Despite what you've done, I believe you're a good person at heart."

He bowed his head and closed his eyes, making sure to appear humble. "Maybe now. Maybe prison has changed me."

"You know something? I like you. And I've never said that to anyone I've interviewed before."

"If you like me so much, leave what you learned about Paula out of the book." He lifted his head, stared in her eyes. "Please, Alexandra. I'm begging you."

She leaned forward, smiled. "If I do, what could you possibly offer me in exchange?"

"What do you want?"

"For starters, I want the whole story between the two of you, all of it." She stood. "For now, I'll go. Leave you to think about it. Let me know what you decide."

CHAPTER 31

Elias Pratt
January 24, 1986

THE MOVE ELIAS WAS ABOUT TO MAKE WAS A RISKY one. He was about to give Alexandra a sliver of truth, hoping she'd keep her word, even though he didn't believe she would. Additional measures needed to be in place. A plan.

His execution had been stayed again.

He had time.

He also had the perfect plan.

Alexandra's book wouldn't be published until after he was dead. She'd said to do so any earlier would be like telling a story and leaving out the ending. Unsure of how long the process would take, she'd met with subjects for other projects in the interim.

"Why leave the truth about Paula out of the book?" Alexandra asked. "Why is it so important to you?"

"Paula was my girlfriend," Elias replied.

Alexandra's eyes widened. "Excuse me? When? For how long?"

"We started seeing each other about six months before I was arrested."

"Why hasn't anyone mentioned this before? Who else knows?"

"No one else knows except Paula, her parents, and now you."

"Why not? Why hide it?"

"Paula's father didn't approve of our relationship. He thought I was too old for her. I guess the four years' difference seems bigger when you're young. He found out, demanded I stop seeing her."

"Did you?"

"Of course not. You think I'd let some ignorant ass keep me from what I want?"

"So you snuck around."

"For a while," he said.

"And then?"

"He caught us one night in her bed." Elias laughed, winked at Alexandra. "Guess we weren't being as quiet as we thought we were. You know how it goes."

"What did her father do?"

"The man was mad as hell. I thought he was going to drive a knife right through me. He tossed my clothes at my face, told me to get out, and said if I ever saw his daughter again, he'd have me arrested for sex with a minor."

"Did you end it then?"

"Are you kidding? That girl was like a juicy slice of forbidden fruit. The more her father tried to keep me away, the more I wanted her."

Elias smiled as he watched Alexandra writhe in her seat, crossing one leg over the other, uncrossing them, and then crossing them back on the other side. It was awkward tension. Sexual tension. He lived life by his own rules, according to what suited him, and Alexandra, with her tight clothes and defiant nature, breathed it in like a window being cracked open in a stuffy room that hadn't been open in ages.

"Did Paula know about your criminal activity?"

He shook his head. "She's a sweet girl. I didn't want to trouble her with such things. She wouldn't have understood my need for ... well, a more exciting life."

"When did you stop seeing her?"

"A couple months before I was arrested, her father found a note I'd left Paula in her room. He knew then we'd never stopped seeing each other, and he decided to try a different approach."

"Which was?"

"He invited me over for dinner, told Paula he may have misjudged me, and wanted to give me another chance."

"You must have been thrilled."

"At first. The family dinners, the 'welcoming me with open arms' attitude, it worked for Paula. It just didn't work for me."

"Why not?"

"Once I was accepted by her parents, the relationship lost its shine. It wasn't risky and forbidden anymore. I became bored, and Paula's father got his daughter back, which I expect is what he'd hoped would happen all along. I broke it off, and she hated me for it."

"You're saying she hated you so much she decided to tell the police you raped her?"

He nodded. "I figured it was her way of getting back at me for breaking her heart. Not long after I was incarcerated, she wrote me a letter, apologizing. She offered to confess what she'd done, make things right."

"Why didn't she?"

"I told her not to. I didn't need her to do that for me. It wouldn't change anything."

Alexandra leaned in. "I appreciate you trusting me with this story, but we're just getting started."

CHAPTER 32

Present Day

THE NEXT MORNING, MY CELL PHONE BUZZED. THE number was local. I leaned over, tried to grab the phone, but my fine motor skills hadn't kicked in yet. The phone slid off the nightstand onto the floor. I bent over the bed, reached down, tried again. "Hello?"

Porter Wells's voice boomed through the phone. "Have you seen Chelsea? Is she with you?"

"Of course not," I replied. "It's seven in the morning. Why would she be here?"

"You're not lying to me to protect her, right?"

"I'm hanging up now," I said.

"Wait."

"Why? I'm obviously a liar. She's been here all night. We had a slumber party."

"I'm sorry. It's just … I can't find her. She's not here. She's not picking up. I'm worried."

I wasn't. I knew she had an officer assigned to watch her. Still, why did my stomach feel queasy? "The last time I saw her was yesterday at

Alexandra's funeral. Why did you think she was with me?"

"I overheard her last night on the phone, talking to her fiancé. She said she was going to call you. She needed to talk to you about something."

"Did she say what she wanted to tell me?"

"No."

Now who was lying?

"We got into another argument last night," he continued. "It was bad. Worse than the others."

"What was the fight over?"

"She said she didn't want to be part of my life anymore. I was angry. I left, went to a hotel. I returned to the house this morning. She was gone, and the house was destroyed."

"When you say *destroyed*—"

"I mean the place has been torn apart. Drawers pulled out, dumped over, shelves emptied. Chelsea's been pissed at me for weeks, but *this* ... this is ridiculous. To desecrate her mother's house just because she's angry, or grieving, or whatever the hell she's going through right now is—"

"How do you know it was Chelsea who trashed the house?" I asked.

"Who else could have done it?"

"Porter, I'm going to give Murphy a call. I'll call you back."

I hung up the phone and dialed Murphy. He answered on the second ring.

"The officer you assigned to Chelsea," I started. "When did you hear from him last?"

"I'm not sure," Murphy said. "I'm headed into work now. Why? What's happened?"

I relayed my conversation with Porter.

When I finished, he said, "Huh, hang on a second. I'll get an answer for you." I waited for him to return to the line. "You're sure you haven't seen Chelsea?"

"Of course I'm sure," I said. "Why?"

"Open your door."

"Why?"

"Just do it, Miss Jax."

I walked to the door, opened it, and found Chelsea standing on the other side dressed in jeans and a puffy pink coat. Her fist was clenched like she was about to knock. In her hand she held a thin, black planner. Standing next to her was her fiancé and the officer assigned to keep an eye on her. The officer held a phone to his ear.

I looked at Chelsea. "Your father just called me. He's really worried about you."

"He doesn't need to worry. I can take care of myself." She thumbed to her left. "Plus, I have this guy."

"What are you doing here?" I asked.

She paused. "We need to talk. Can I come in?"

CHAPTER 33

CHELSEA'S FIANCÉ HELD HIS HAND OUT TO ME. "IT'S nice to meet you, Joss. I'm Bradley. Chelsea has told me so much about you."

It seemed strange for a boy of his age to show this kind of respect, given the loose, relaxed nature of most millennials his age. But everything about Bradley was different, from his perfectly combed hair to his tight, white slacks and fitted, gray wool jacket. He oozed money and good breeding.

I accepted his soft, *never worked a day in his privileged life* hand in mine, and we shook. "Nice to meet you too. I hear you and Chelsea are getting married in a few weeks."

"We were," he clarified. "With the death of her mother, my family decided it would be best to put it off for a few months at least."

I found his comment revealing. He and Chelsea hadn't decided together. His family had decided for them. "Who are your parents?"

He beamed. "Hollis and Dorothy Claiborne."

I drew a blank, which he happily filled in for me. "Governor Hollis Claiborne."

Impressive.

"We've never met."

He gave me a snarky look like, *Why would you?*

Chelsea fanned herself with a hand. "Man, it's like a million degrees in here." She removed her coat, adjusted the sleeve of her shirt that had slid off her shoulder, and we all sat down. Chelsea tapped the top of the table with her fingers like it was a piano. Whatever she'd come to say, she still seemed unsure about saying it. Not one for awkward silence, I helped things along. "What do you need to talk to me about?"

"I, umm, lied to you the other day," she said.

I knew this already, of course. "Okay. What about?"

"When we first met, you asked me if I knew about the book my mother was writing before she died. I said I didn't. Truth is ... I do know something about it."

"I know."

Her eyes widened. "How could you?"

"Before we got on the subject of your mother's book, you didn't have a problem looking me in the eye. Afterward, you did. Why did you feel like you couldn't tell me what you knew?"

Chelsea rolled an elastic band off her wrist, fastening it around her hair into a ponytail. "My mom had just died. I didn't know you. Not really. I didn't see the point in talking about it. After I was run off the road yesterday, I feel differently. I'm willing to say anything just to feel safe again."

"What can you tell me about the book your mom was writing?"

"It was going to be her last. This was one reason why she didn't tell anyone she was writing it. And it's just ... I've had time to think about it the last few days. I'm worried she was killed because someone found out what she wrote in it."

"Who else knew about the book?"

"No one, except me, and my dad probably knows now too. That's why we were fighting last night. He has her laptop, and he won't give it to me."

"How do you know he has it?" I asked. "Did he admit it to you?"

She shook her head. "It was in the top drawer of my mom's desk. A drawer she *always* kept locked. I was walking by the desk last night and noticed the metal hole the key goes into looked funny. It was bent, like someone jammed a knife inside the hole and broke it. I ran my finger over the hole, and the drawer pulled right open. The laptop wasn't there."

"Did you ask your dad if he had it?"

She nodded. "He swore he didn't have it. He's lying. I know he does."

"Is that why you trashed your mom's house after he left, to find the laptop?"

She jerked her head back. "Trashed the house? What are you talking about?"

"Your father said when he returned home this morning, it was a disaster. Someone broke in last night. Your father has been trying to find you. He seems genuinely worried."

Chelsea sprung from the chair. "Are you kidding? Someone broke into my mother's house?! When? Did they take anything? Do the police know about it?!"

"I'm not sure. If it wasn't you and it wasn't your father—"

"How could it be me? I wasn't there." She looked at the officer. "Ask the police guy. He'll tell you."

The officer nodded.

"When did you leave the house?" I asked.

"Last night. I thought after my dad cooled off, he'd come back, try to talk to me again. I couldn't go another round with him. So I left, went to Bradley's parents' house. I didn't leave there until this morning, and I came straight here to see you. I haven't been home since I left last night."

"It's true," Bradley said. "She got to my house around eight."

Chelsea grabbed Bradley's hand, walked to the door. "I … I can't be here right now. I have to go."

"Hang on, Chelsea," I said. "Give me one minute, okay? I understand you're shook up, but maybe if you give me more information, the two of us can figure out who broke into your house and why."

She fidgeted with the key in her hand, sliding her thumb up and down like a nervous tic. "It's just ... the thought of someone in my mother's house ... all of this ... it's so hard. I'm not even safe in my own house anymore."

Sensing she was about to cry, Bradley squeezed her hand. "It's all right, babe. We'll go back to the house, pack some bags, and you can stay with me until we're married. My mom has already offered for you to stay with us as long as you want. Say what you came here to say."

Chelsea sighed, looked at me. "Okay, fine. Just ... let's hurry."

I picked the black planner off the table, held it out to her. "You left this on the table."

"Oh, right. I meant to leave it. I brought it here to give to you. Well, loan to you."

I opened the planner, flipped through it.

"That's my mom's planner," Chelsea said.

"Where did you get it?" I asked.

"It was in my mom's desk."

"Wouldn't the police have taken it when they searched the house?"

She nodded. "After what happened to my mom, I wanted to look through it first. I gave it to Bradley, and he kept it at his house until now."

"You should have turned it in," I said.

"I am kinda, now. I'm giving it to you."

"I'm not the police. Have you looked through it?"

She nodded. "I went through her appointments last night, but I can't make heads or tails of anything. I was hoping you could take a look. Maybe you'll see something different."

"Absolutely, but I need to be honest. After I look at it, I want to hand it over to the police so they can look at it as well."

"I brought it to you because I don't want it given to them. They still have the purse she was carrying the night she died. They also took other things from her car. I have no idea when I'll get any of it back. My dad asked, and they told him they didn't know either."

"Trust me, giving them the planner is the right thing to do, Chelsea. We're all trying to accomplish the same thing here."

She frowned. "Whatever. I guess."

"I'll go through it first just to see if anything stands out."

She opened the hotel room door, looked back. "Thank you. Will you tell me if you find anything?"

I nodded. "One last question before you leave. You never said whether you know the subject of your mother's last book. Do you know? Did she tell you?"

"She didn't, but I was in her office one day when she was writing. I was at her desk talking to her, and I recognized a name she'd typed."

"What name?"

Her answer was shocking and unexpected, spinning me in a whole new direction.

Elias Pratt.

CHAPTER 34

I SPENT THE NEXT HOUR PORING OVER THE APPOINTMENT book, piecing together whether or not Elias Pratt and Alexandra Weston's murder could somehow be connected. Several things didn't add up in my mind. For one, Elias was dead. For another, Alexandra had just released a book about him. Still, it was odd Chelsea had seen her mother typing Elias's name.

Alexandra's appointment book listed her various engagements, but there was one glaring problem. The individual name of the person she met with on any given day was almost impossible to decipher. Most of the entries were initials in place of people's actual names. So much secrecy. No wonder Chelsea couldn't make sense of it.

Aside from a few meetings with Barbara Berry, I focused on two of the names I believed she'd written as initials in the book: SH and LP. I picked up my copy of the book Alexandra Weston had signed for me, cross-referenced it with the initials, and came up with two matching names: Sandra Hamilton and Loretta Pratt, Elias's mother.

I closed the appointment book and set it down.

Finch entered the room. "Any luck?"

"Maybe. I'm more confused now than I was before."

He bent down, picked something off the floor, handed it to me. "What's this?"

I look at the item. An old photo. "I don't know. There's a sleeve in the back of Alexandra's appointment book. It must have fallen from there."

Finch stared at the photo. "Who do you think the guy is in the picture? He doesn't look a thing like Porter."

I was about ninety-percent sure I knew. "My guess, Elias Pratt, but I've never seen this photo before. It wasn't in the first book she published about him, and it's not in her latest one either."

I scrutinized the photo further. It was small, folded to about a quarter of its original size. There wasn't a name on it, but there was a year. 1982. A year before he was arrested. In the photo, Elias was smiling, holding a puppy in his arms. Wearing a simple white tank top and jeans, he looked innocent, his eyes kind and merciful, unlike the heartless killer he turned out to be. I rubbed a thumb across his face, studying his features, and that was when I recognized something I'd seen before.

CHAPTER 35

I WAS HEADING OUT OF MY HOTEL ROOM WHEN MY cell phone rang. Seeing the name on the caller ID caused me to tense, and for a moment, it felt as though I had no more breath in my body. He was a blast from the past. Someone I hadn't heard from in years.

"I can't do this right now," I said into the phone. "I can't talk to you, Lucas. It's not a good time."

"Sure you can," Lucas said. "Try."

His voice sounded exactly the same as I remembered. I wondered if he thought the same about me.

"Joslyn, you still there?" he asked.

"Don't call me that. In fact, don't call me at all."

I pushed the end button, tossed the phone onto the bed. Twenty seconds later, it rang again, just like I knew it would. I watched it buzz once, then twice. On the third time, I cursed at the phone and then answered it. "I said not to call me."

"If you don't want to talk to me, why do you keep answering?"

Unnerving, irritating ass.

"What do you want, Lucas?"

"You decide if you're coming to Clay and Court's wedding next weekend?"

"It's none of your business."

"Maybe not. Wanted you to know, if you wanna come, it's fine by me. I actually think it would be a good thing."

"It's *fine* with you?" I said. "I don't need your permission."

"Saw your mom today at the store. She seemed upset, said she didn't think you were gonna make it. She is really hoping you'll be here."

I envisioned the rendezvous between Lucas and my mother in my mind—how it went, how they talked to each other, how many times my mother mentioned things like how sorry she was when our marriage ended. After all he'd put me through, the fact she still had a soft spot for him irked me.

"My conversations with my mother are also none of your business," I said. "You shouldn't be talking to her to me."

"You have it all wrong, you know. She approached me, Joslyn. Not the other way around. I'm just sayin', don't stay away on account of me."

"I don't base *any* of my decisions on you. I stopped needing your permission a long time ago."

"Good."

"Good," I said.

"Anyway, been a long time. It would be nice to see you again."

I wanted to say, *Yeah, well, it wouldn't be good to see YOU.* The words were right there, dancing around the tip of my tongue like a fighter dodging his opponent in a boxing ring. I opened my mouth then closed it. I didn't need to do this. Nothing I said would change the past or affect the future. The "us" had dissipated long ago.

"If you're worried about Kinsey being there, she won't."

"It makes no difference to me if she is or if she isn't. Why would it?"

"I mean to say, she won't be there because we're not together anymore. We're divorced."

There it was at last. The clarity I needed for his unexpected phone call shifted into focus. He may have used my mother as the excuse for his call, but he had another agenda. He was alone, and being alone terrified him. "What are you trying to do by calling me—"

"I'm not trying to do anything. I thought … I mean, I was hoping we could be friends."

"Friends? We're not friends, Lucas."

"Why can't we be?"

"A friend is someone I can count on. Someone I can trust. Someone who would never betray me. You're none of these things."

"Come on, Joss, I'm trying here."

"I'm sorry. It just isn't possible. After all that's happened, I can't let you back in. It would be too hard."

I pressed the end button again.

And this time when the phone rang again, I exercised restraint.

CHAPTER 36

WE WERE JUST ABOUT TO ROUND THE CORNER LEADING
to Porter's house when I glanced in my car's side-view mirror for the
tenth time. For the past several minutes, the car behind us had
taken the same turns Finch had. He'd noticed too. I could tell. But
he hadn't said anything. Glancing in the car's mirror, I didn't have
the best view of the man in the car behind us, but in my own
paranoia, I saw my stalker. The truth was, I'd seen him over and
over and over again since Clara died. Only, it wasn't ever him. He
was the clerk at the store, the guy at the gym, the onlooker in my
live studio audience.

It's not him, Joss. Pull yourself together. It's not him.

Finch parked in front of Porter's house, and the car behind us
passed by. The man turned and smiled, then used a garage door
opener to open the garage three houses down.

The front door opened before we got to it.

"Where's Chelsea?" I asked.

Porter stood in the doorway, his arms folded, face all screwed
up like he didn't want to see me. The feeling was mutual.

"Not here."

Perfect. Exactly what I hoped he would say.

"You received my text earlier when Chelsea stopped by my hotel, right?" I asked.

"I did."

"And the one about where she was last night?"

He nodded.

"Have you notified the police about the break-in last night?"

He laughed. "Are you kidding? I knew if I didn't, you would have. It seems you have your hand in every kind of jar there is in this town. Must be nice to use your celebrity to get what you want."

"You know all about using people to get what you want," I said.

"What's your point?"

My *point* was about to be made clear.

I leaned to the side, looking past him into the house. A few cardboard boxes were stacked in the corner of the living room. "Are you moving out?"

"What does it look like?"

"And Chelsea, she's staying?"

He turned a hand up. "This is *her* house now. Not mine. She's made that clear. If we're to have any relationship at all, I need to give her what she wants."

"Aren't you concerned about her safety after what happened yesterday?"

He laughed. "Would it matter if I was? My daughter informed me that if I'm here, she won't be. So what would you like me to do, Miss Jax? Camp out in my car in the driveway to ensure her safety? She has a uniformed officer for that. Not to mention a fiancé."

I stepped into the house. Finch followed.

"As of this moment, I still live here," Porter said. "And I haven't invited you in."

"Where's Alexandra's laptop?"

"How should I know? I told you what happened to this place. Look around. First the cops go through it, then it gets burglarized."

"When did police search the house?"

"Tuesday."

"I'm assuming they never found a laptop."

No reply.

"Are you sure you have nothing to say? I may not know who broke in here, but I believe you're the one who has Alexandra's laptop."

He palmed his cell phone like he was going to make a call. "You know something? I've had enough."

Finch eyed Porter's phone like he was prepared to jack it from his hand as soon as a button was pressed, which may not have been such a bad thing. Still, I had a better idea.

"Before you decide whether or not you're actually going to make a call, I'd like to show you something." I reached into my back pocket, pulled out the photo, held it in front of Porter's face.

"What am I looking at?" he asked.

"Elias Pratt. Don't you recognize him?"

"Of course I do. Who wouldn't? *Why* are you showing his picture to me?"

"I found this photo tucked away inside Alexandra's appointment book."

"Her planner? How did you get—"

"Chelsea gave it to me this morning. She thinks Alexandra was writing another book about Elias Pratt. Is that true?"

"I don't know. I think so. I assumed she was, at least. Though I couldn't understand why."

"When did you find out about her new book?"

"I overheard a conversation between Alex and Paula Page."

"On the phone?" I asked.

"Here, at the house."

He was quite the gifted eavesdropper.

"When did the conversation between Alexandra and Paula occur?"

"Right before Alex left on her book tour, Paula showed up at the house in a frantic, crazed state, shouting at Alex to 'leave things alone.' She was hysterical."

"Any idea what things she was referring to?"

"Alex was planning to expose something about Paula in her new book. She told Paula it was too late, said Paula should have told the truth in the first place. She wouldn't be in the situation she was in if she had."

The truth about what? I wondered.

"How did Paula react to Alexandra's response?"

"Paula threatened her, said if she didn't back down, she'd expose a secret she knew about Alex too."

"How did the visit end?"

"Paula shouted a few expletives at Alex and left. I walked into the room a minute later, asked what it was all about, and Alex laughed, acted like it was nothing. She was rattled though. I could tell."

It was clear to me now. "Elias Pratt is the reason you broke into Alexandra's desk drawer and removed the laptop."

He laughed like my assumption was absurd. "Why would I do that?"

"You wanted to read what she'd written. What she'd revealed in the book."

"I've never given a damn about what she puts in those books. Why would this one be any different?"

"I've been doing a lot of thinking today," I said. "Ever since you admitted Alexandra gave you cash to keep you from blabbing about the divorce, something's been bothering me."

"Yeah? What's that?"

"Paying you not to mention the divorce to Chelsea before she was married doesn't make sense. Many people already assumed the relationship between you and Alexandra was failing. Even Chelsea. Alexandra *did* pay you though, didn't she? She just paid you for a different reason."

He remained silent. I continued.

"Take a good look at this picture of Elias Pratt. What do you see?"

"What everyone sees. A killer. A pathetic man who deserved to die, and he did."

"You want to know what I see?"

"Whatever you're getting at, say it."

I set the photo on the kitchen counter, stabbed my finger onto the noticeable birthmark on Elias's shoulder. "You're not Chelsea's real father, are you?"

CHAPTER 37

"OF COURSE I'M CHELSEA'S FATHER," PORTER SAID. "What are you trying to do here?"

"Look at this photo of Elias," I said. "Really look at it. The shape of his eyes, his complexion, the way his upper lip curves a little more on his right side when he smiles. It's subtle, but if you really look, you can see the similarities."

He stared at the photo, said nothing.

I took my phone out of my pocket. "Let's call Chelsea. When she gets here, we'll show her the photo and see what she thinks."

Porter pressed a hand to his chest, patting himself once, twice, then three times. I waited, gave him time to catch his breath.

"Let's sit down," he said. "But first, I need a drink."

He walked into the kitchen, removing three glasses and an unopened bottle of whiskey from a cabinet. He filled each glass half full, passed them around.

"Thanks," I said, when he handed a glass to me, "but I don't—"

"Don't be a prude, Miss Jax. Drink the damn thing. Okay?"

I hated whiskey—the pungent smell, the peaty taste—but I downed it in one giant swig anyway, hoping he wouldn't offer me another. Finch set his glass on the counter, whiskey still inside. Porter drank the glass he'd poured for himself, reached for Finch's, and drank it too.

"This is three-thousand-dollar whiskey," Porter said to Finch. "If you can't appreciate it, I sure as hell am not letting it go to waste."

Porter grabbed the whiskey bottle and held it out in front of him, allowing the bottle to lead the way to the living room. The three of us filed in and sat down.

"Does Chelsea know you're not her father?" I asked.

He sighed. "Before I reply to your question, what makes you think she isn't?"

"When she was at my hotel earlier, she was adjusting the sleeve of her shirt, and I noticed a birthmark on her shoulder. The same birthmark in the photo I just showed you."

"What do you plan to do if I tell you the truth?"

"If you're asking if I have any intention of revealing it to anyone else, I don't. Not unless I have to. Does Chelsea know?"

He shook his head. "She doesn't, and I don't know you enough to know if I can trust you."

Whether he could or couldn't, he no longer had a choice.

"You can trust her," Finch said. "Joss would never lie to you, especially about this."

Porter looked at Finch like it didn't matter; he didn't believe *him* either. "It's a hard question to answer. I'm her father. I'm just not her biological father."

"How do you know Chelsea doesn't know?"

"Because her mother and I worked hard to keep it that way. It was one of the only things we agreed on actually."

"How long have you known?"

Porter tipped the whiskey container, poured himself another drink, stared at an abstract painting on the wall of two girls stretching on a parallel bar in ballet class. His expression was disheartened, as if recalling an unwanted memory. "Chelsea was around five years old when I learned the truth about who her father really was. By then, we'd already bonded. She was mine. Still is."

"How did you find out? Did Alexandra admit it to you?"

He shook his head. "I doubt Alex would have ever told me unless there was an advantage for her to do so."

"How did you figure it out then?" I asked.

"Chelsea's always had that half-inch birthmark on her shoulder. Looks like a bird in flight. I never thought much of it, just assumed it was a strange little oddity some kids have. One day Alexandra was going through some old files in her office. A folder fell on the floor. Pictures slipped out, scattered everywhere. I bent down, helped her pick them up. And that's when I saw it."

"Saw what?"

"A photo of Elias Pratt. One I hadn't ever seen before. The one you just showed me. I noticed the same thing you did. He had the exact same birthmark in the exact same place."

"Did you confront Alexandra?"

"It wasn't necessary. She saw the look on my face and she knew there was no point denying it. For years I'd raised Chelsea thinking she was my daughter because the woman I loved, the woman who was supposed to be my confidant and best friend, thought it was better to lie to me than tell me the truth. You want to know the saddest part? She never would have told me if I hadn't discovered it for myself."

It was a despicable secret, and I knew why Alexandra had done it. If the public ever found out about the baby's true father, they'd also find out about her wrongdoings. She probably would have never had an interview with a man behind bars again. Her perfect image, the one she worked so hard to develop over the years, would have been marred forever.

"How did Alexandra manage to be intimate with Elias when he was locked up?" I asked.

He tipped his glass in my direction. "According to Alexandra, there are ways around everything. Even in prison."

But Elias wasn't just in prison. He was on death row.

"Was it a one-time thing?"

"She said it was, but then, she was a gifted liar, wasn't she?"

"In your opinion, were there genuine feelings between Alexandra and Elias?"

He nodded. "Until the day he fried, and even then it didn't stop. She visited his grave once a month for ten years. She didn't know I knew, but I did."

He downed another shot, set the glass down, poured another. I exchanged glances with Finch, neither of us saying a word. For days, I'd despised Porter, convincing myself he was a manipulator, a person who used Alexandra for her money, flaunting his relationships with other women in her face for his own amusement while extorting her on the side. Now I wasn't sure who he was or if I'd misjudged him.

"What happened *after* you found out the truth about Chelsea?" I asked.

"Alexandra begged me to stay in the marriage, to give us another chance. Not because she loved me, and not because she was sorry, but because she wanted to keep our perfect illusion of a life intact. How could I after her betrayal?"

"If you felt that way, why didn't you file for divorce and move on with your life?"

"I thought about it. Almost went through with it a couple of times. It's like I said before. Chelsea wasn't mine by blood, but to me, she was still my little girl. If we divorced, Alex would have done everything in her power to keep Chelsea away from me, even if it hurt Chelsea in the process. It would have been her way of making me pay for not giving her what she wanted."

I thought about Alexandra, about how different people could be when the veil was lifted. Once the true identity was revealed, the perfect picture took on a stain that couldn't be removed.

"What about the money she was giving you?" I asked.

"I wasn't extorting money from her. Early in the marriage, before I found out about Chelsea, I used some of the money I made from my own accounting business on investments. At the time, I tried to involve Alexandra in those investments. She had no interest. *That's* what I've been living on all these years. Aside from the regular bills any couple has, I haven't asked that woman for a dime in ages."

"You would rather have me believe you were a womanizer, interested in Alexandra's money, than be honest with me?"

"If it kept the truth from coming out, yes. Chelsea may act like she hates me right now, but she'll come around. She always does."

"Why did Alexandra go to so much effort to paint you like a villain?" I asked. "She tried turning Chelsea against you."

"Alexandra was in love with Roland Sinclair. She planned to marry him."

"How? He's already married."

"Not many know this, but his wife is dying. I don't believe she'll be around in three months. Alexandra planned to be there for him after his wife died. In my opinion, this was the reason she was writing one last book. She was burnt out on the whole process. They would have finally been free to build a life together."

"And Chelsea? When did Alex plan to give her the news?"

"After Chelsea's marriage, but Alex had already planted the seed, telling Chelsea I've been with other women, making me look bad so she would despise me and welcome Roland into her life when the time came. Alex probably hoped Chelsea would see Roland as some kind of savior to her grieving mother."

"How long have you known about Alexandra's plans with Roland?"

"A couple weeks."

"You know how bad that sounds, right?" I said.

"I do."

"You're the one with the most compelling motive, the one person who needed Alexandra dead the most."

"I just told you the truth, and I believe you know that. I also believe you no longer think I had anything to do with her death, because I didn't."

Telling me what he thought I should believe didn't make me certain of his innocence. I wasn't sure of anything anymore. "Even if you didn't kill your wife, I'm still convinced you took her laptop."

Porter stood, walked into another room, returning seconds later with a gray laptop clutched in his hand. "I took this the night before the police came to search the house, so I could read the book Alexandra had written."

"Why?"

"The person who killed Alex is now going after my daughter. If something she'd written was tied to Alex's murder, I wanted to know about it."

"What can you tell me about the book?" I asked.

"Nothing."

"What do you mean? You're holding the laptop. You must have found something."

"I knew the password to get into Alex's computer, but the book file is protected. I can't get into it."

"Who else knew about the book?" I asked.

"Barbara Berry."

"Anyone else?"

"I don't know. Roland possibly, and then whomever she talked to or interviewed prior to her death."

"Barbara Berry told me she didn't know what the book was about," I said.

He laughed. "Of course she did. The woman is a liar."

"How can you be sure?"

"Trust me. Alex would have told her agent."

I recalled my previous conversation with Barbara. If she knew about Alexandra's book, what else was she hiding? I thought about the two names written on the piece of paper Barbara gave me. "Barbara suggested you killed Alexandra."

He cocked his head back, laughed. "Witch. Doesn't surprise me."

"She also suggested Doyle Eldridge."

Porter swished a hand through the air. "Doyle's harmless. He'd never hurt Alex. He's just a longtime fan with a crush."

"Maybe. Either way, you need to turn Alexandra's laptop over to the police. They can open the file, figure out what's really in that book. Take it in, give it to Detective Murphy."

"And I'm just supposed to trust he'll keep his mouth shut if the book contains what I think it does?"

"Tell him your concerns. I believe you can count on him to be discreet. I'd also like you to think about talking to Chelsea. She's going through a lot right now, but the way things are going, I believe the truth is going to come out. You don't want it coming from someone other than you."

He nodded several times, entwined his fingers over one knee. "I'll think about it. In the meantime, here's something you should think about. Barbara Berry lied to you and then tried to get you to believe I had something to do with Alex's murder. Maybe you need to ask yourself why."

CHAPTER 38

I LEFT PORTER'S HOUSE UNCERTAIN WHETHER HE WAS father of the year or if he was much more cunning, a man with a gift of spinning things in his favor. I'd started to feel like a pointer on a board game, whirring around and around before stopping on a color which sent me in a whole new direction. I'd started out determined to find Alexandra's killer. Now, the more I knew about her, the more disgusted I was. I questioned my motives for deciding to stay, deciding it all came down to one thing: curiosity.

Given my questionable trust in Porter, I called Murphy, gave him a heads-up on the laptop. I kept my word and didn't mention Chelsea. Not just for Porter's benefit, but for hers too.

In the spirit of sharing, Murphy told me the fingerprints found at the scene where Louis Massey died led police to the home of Bucky Fox, a thief known for pimping hot merchandise on the street. Turned out, Louis's death wasn't connected to Alexandra. He died for showing off, running his mouth to the wrong people. It reminded me of a quote I once read by Napoleon Hill. "Money without brains is always dangerous."

CHAPTER 39

AN HOUR LATER, I HUDDLED NEXT TO FINCH AS WE walked through a frigid park where Doyle Eldridge's son told us his dad liked to go after his daily walk to the coffee shop. Nine benches and several mistaken identities later, we found Doyle leaning against a bald cypress, his head buried in the pages of a Patricia Cornwell book about Jack the Ripper. He sensed our presence, wiped his eyes, and looked up.

"Hello, Miss Jax," he said. "I knew you'd come."

"How?"

"I've been keeping an eye on things."

"What does that mean?"

"It doesn't matter."

"It *does* matter," Finch said. "She asked you a question. Answer it."

"Would you like to know a fun fact?" Doyle asked. "I've known Alexandra since grade school. We were in the same class in the first and fourth grades, you see. My family moved away when school ended after my fourth year, and we lost touch for a while until I moved back again in the eleventh grade. I'll never forget the day we sat in English class when she looked at me and said she was going to be a famous writer one day."

He definitely was odd. With each reply, his head bobbed around like there wasn't enough support to hold it up.

"If Alexandra has known you all these years, why didn't she ever tell anyone?"

"Why was it important for them to know? It was no one's business. I guess you could say I was a confidant, someone she could talk to like she would a girlfriend. She didn't have any of those, but she always had me."

What she *had* was a plethora of hidden doors, each containing its own unique secret.

"Barbara Berry didn't see you as Alexandra's friend. She saw you as her stalker."

He shrugged. "I know."

"And?"

"She's entitled to her opinion. It doesn't make it true."

"It doesn't make it a lie either. Did you give Alexandra a scrapbook where you'd pasted your head and Alexandra's head onto a bride and groom?"

He beamed with pride. "Matter of fact, I did."

"Why?"

He snapped shut the book he was holding, stood, folded his arms in front of him. "I don't see how answering any of your questions is going to help you find what you're really after."

"It might. You were obsessed with Alexandra. Isn't that true?"

"Wasn't everyone?"

"*Everyone* didn't take the time to make her a scrapbook," I said. "You did. Did you love her?"

He nodded. "I did."

"Must have been hard when you found out she was in love with someone else."

"If you mean Mr. Sinclair, I've known about him for years. And you're right. It would have been grand if she had loved me the way I loved her, but she didn't. I pasted our faces into the scrapbook to remind her of something she once gave to me when we were in grade school. Just a little card one Valentine's Day. I wanted to know if she still remembered. She did."

"Where were you the night she was murdered?" I asked.

"At home, with my son, just like I told police."

"All night?"

"All night. The love I had for Alexandra was the kind of love a brother has for his sister, not a man for a woman. It wasn't sexual, and it wasn't wrong."

Aside from his odd behavior, which I assumed may have just been the way he'd always been, I believed him. "Thank you for giving me a few minutes of your time."

"You came all this way to talk to me and you're not even going to ask me about the book?"

"What book?"

"The one Alexandra was writing when she died."

"How do you know about it?"

"I told you, we were friends. She knew she could talk to me about anything and I'd keep quiet."

"Who was the subject of the book?"

"She was."

"Alexandra?"

He nodded.

"I don't follow. She writes about criminals, just like I do. Why would she be the subject of her own book?"

He raised a brow. "You're assuming the book was the same kind she'd written before. It wasn't. It was the story of her life. Her memoir."

CHAPTER 40

Elias Pratt
December 27, 1989

OVER THE LAST SEVERAL YEARS, ELIAS HAD GROWN accustomed to the eye candy Alexandra provided during each visit, her titillating style of dress, her sassy *I pretend to care but I really don't* attitude. On the outside, she was bold and brazen; yet a softer more vulnerable side lingered, a side concealed from everyone except him.

Piece by piece, Alexandra's hardened shell had chipped away the more they saw each other. Small clues at first, like the way she sheepishly looked down when he said something that made her blush, or when she tucked a few strands of her hair behind her ear when his eyes lingered on hers for too long. The formalities of the past were gone. He was no longer referred to as Mr. Pratt. He was Elias. She was Alexa. And he'd achieved exactly what he wanted.

Today when he saw her, everything about her was off, different, like she was a changed person. She wore black from head to toe, her supple flesh covered with a turtleneck beneath a frumpy cardigan sweater.

It wasn't like her.

It wasn't like her at all.

She made no eye contact before sitting across from him, spoke no pleasantries, offered no greeting.

"What's wrong, Alexa?" he asked.

She cleared her throat, furrowed her brow. "Nothing. I don't have a lot of time today, Elias."

"What's eating you? Tell me."

"Nothing. It's nothing. Everything's fine."

Except it wasn't.

"Are those *tears* in your eyes?"

They *were* tears.

She breathed heavily, struggling to keep her composure in front of him. Aware he understood what was happening, she bit her lower lip like the gesture would prevent an onslaught of water from dripping down her face.

But a tear did drop.

Then another.

Then the floodgates opened.

She was in full-blown, meltdown mode—a magnificent sight to see.

Everything he'd wanted, everything he'd hoped for was finally coming true.

"Talk to me," he said. "Tell me what's wrong. Are you upset because we've reached the end? We both knew the time would come when my last stay of execution would be denied."

She shook her head. "It's not that."

He didn't believe her.

What else *could* it be?

"I've made my peace, prayed to whatever god will listen," he said.

Using the sleeve of her sweater, she wiped the tears from her face. "Dammit! I can't do this today, Elias. I'm sorry. I have to go."

She stood halfway up, then sat back down again. Pressing a hand to her stomach, she closed her eyes, slowed her breathing.

"What the hell's going on with you today?" he asked.

Without opening her eyes, she said, "I'm not feeling well."

"Go home. Get some rest."

"No! This may be the last time I'll see you again before they … before you …"

She couldn't say it.

Before he died.

Fourteen days.

Fourteen days and it would be all over.

"It's going to be okay, you know," he said.

"It's not going to be okay."

"Sure it is. You'll finally publish your book, and I'll be … well, in hell if you believe in such things."

She thrust a hand over her mouth, but it was too late. Pieces of semi-processed food erupted, spraying the room. Elias threw his hands up, pushed his chair backward. An armed guard rushed to Alexandra's side. She tried pushing him away, but he took her by the arm anyway. "Miss, let me help you."

Alexandra pressed a hand to her stomach, glanced down, then locked eyes with Elias. Reality came into focus, and he saw what he was meant to see.

"Wait a minute. Are you …?"

A slight nod from Alexandra provided the answer.

Alexandra wrenched her arm free, said to the guard, "Call someone to clean this up please."

The guard didn't move.

"Don't think about it," Alexandra pressed. "Do it."

Unsure of how to handle the predicament, the guard kept an eye on Alexandra while backing toward the door. He opened it partway, yelled for help.

"Congratulations," Elias said. "I'm happy for you."

"If that's true, you should be happy for yourself as well," she whispered. "I haven't had sex with my husband in weeks. It isn't his baby, Elias. It's yours."

CHAPTER 41

Alexandra Weston
Ten Minutes Later

ALEXANDRA SAT INSIDE HER CAR IN A PARKING LOT next to the prison. She rarely cried, but today was a rare day. After confirming her pregnancy a couple weeks earlier, she'd had several outbursts like this one. First the denial, then the decision on whether to keep the baby or get rid of it, followed by a plan on how to keep the baby's father a secret, and whether or not she'd tell Elias the truth. One day earlier she'd decided against telling him. Now, having done it minutes before, she drove both fists into the center of her steering wheel and screamed.

Why did you tell him?

Why? Why? Why?

She could question it all she wanted. She knew why. Somehow over the years, she'd fallen in love with him. Even now, it was hard for her to believe. She was a logical woman. A woman who never made the slightest misstep when it came to her career. In all her years as a writer, she'd never allowed the flirtations of her subjects to get in the way of her work before.

Until now.

Until *him*.

He hadn't just made her feel special, and wanted, and whole. He *knew* her. He saw a part of her no one else did. Her family, her husband, the few friends she had, all of them accepted what little she revealed about herself, a single layer in a much more complex, multi-layered person.

Elias was the opposite. He worked his way in, piece by piece, visit after visit, until she felt raw and naked in his presence. She fought her feelings for years until the awareness of knowing their time was coming to an end overshadowed all else. All reason. All logic. Somehow, it no longer mattered.

CHAPTER 42

Present Day

NOW IN HER EIGHTIES, LORETTA PRATT'S TIMEWORN, wrinkled face exhibited a life marred by heartache and despair, each elongated, deep-set wrinkle like crooked lines on a map, connecting one hardship to the next. As I stood there on her front porch, staring for entirely too long, I couldn't help but wonder what else in her life had gone awry, or if the overwhelming loss of her son all those years ago was enough to ebb the beauty and light I was sure she once had.

Loretta barely looked in my direction before waving us into the house. She offered a slight nod then turned, using her cane to lead the way. We followed her into a spotless living room where a single color dominated the sparse décor: white. White piano. White sofa. Furry white rug covering a real hardwood floor. The room had a museum feel to it. Clean. Unstained. Pure. Stodgy.

"My name is Joss Jax," I said. "And this is Finch."

He raised a hand. She blinked, her face otherwise remaining steady. Unchanged. She didn't seem the least bit interested in who we were, or that she'd just welcomed two strangers into her house without inquiring what we were after.

When she finally did speak, her voice was solid, but lacked fluctuation in tone. "What can I do for you two?"

"I'd like to talk to you about your son."

"Which one, Everett or Ethan?"

"Elias."

Her lips formed the slightest smile, her eyes shifting to a picture of a young Elias inside a silver frame over the fireplace mantle. "Oh. Him. What do you want to know?"

"When he was alive, did you visit him in prison?"

"A few times, yes."

"Did he tell you anything about his visits with Alexandra Weston?"

She nodded. "He spoke of her often. Of the book she was writing. Besides me, his lawyer, and our pastor, she was his only other visitor."

I moved to a harder question. "Were you aware of Elias's relationship with Alexandra?"

"If you're going to keep firing questions off like this, I need to sit down." She sat on a chair, crossed one leg over the other, looked at us like it was up for us to decide whether we wanted to remain standing. "When you say relationship, which relationship are you referring to, the professional one or the personal one?"

"You knew about the personal relationship that existed between them?"

"I believe we should clarify what personal means. You do mean sex, don't you?"

I looked at Finch. He looked like he wanted to disappear into the floor.

"Elias was on death row in prison," I said. "I don't see how they managed anything physical between them."

"I don't know. It's not like he'd give those details to his mother. Of course, he always was different from the time he was a young boy. So different from the others. But he was my son, and I loved him anyway."

Her attitude toward him made me wonder if she'd regarded him the same way she did his brothers. If she had not, I was sure it had affected him. "How would it have been possible for Elias and Alexandra to be intimate together? Didn't they conduct their visits through a partition?"

"You didn't know Alexandra Weston very well, did you? Elias always said she was the only woman he'd ever known who could bend any man to her will. Even though Alexandra and Elias had one-on-one visits with a guard present, there were times they were alone."

"How did she manage that?"

"The men at that prison loved her, both inmates and guards alike."

"Do you know if it only happened once, or multiple times?"

"I don't have an exact number. Why does it matter now anyway?"

I wondered what the guard received for giving her what she wanted and looking the other way. I also wondered what made Alexandra want to have sex with Elias in the first place. Were real feelings there? Had she loved him?

"I suppose Alexandra found a way to convince the guard to look the other way, so to speak, give her a few minutes alone with him. Like I said before, she was a woman who always got her way."

And he was the kind of man who slaughtered people.

"Who told you they were intimate with each other?" I asked.

"They both did, though Alexandra didn't mention it to me until recently. I'll never forget the shocked look on her face when she realized I'd known all these years and kept quiet."

"When did you last see Alexandra?" I asked.

"A few months ago."

"And when before that?"

"It had been years. Decades. She showed up at my door, said she was writing a book and wanted to talk to me before she published it. Her exact words were, 'I need to tell you the truth about a few things before you read about it in my book.' Imagine her surprise when she found out I already knew what she'd come to tell me."

"Did Alexandra say why she'd decided to write a memoir?"

"She said after all these years she wanted to come clean about her life. If she didn't, she feared someone else would, and if it was going to be told, she wanted to be the one to tell it."

"Did she mention who she thought would betray her?"

Loretta shook her head. "She only said there would be a chapter in her upcoming memoir devoted to Elias. Decades ago when Alexandra wrote *The Devil Died at Midnight*, she left some details out. I never understood why. The last time I visited Elias, he said she was quite smitten with him. He joked about having manipulated her."

"In what way?"

"I don't know." She paused then added, "I hate to say this, but I'm going to. It's been eating at me for days now, ever since Alexandra Weston died. There's a chance that I'm to blame for her death."

"How? Do you know who did it?"

"Maybe."

I hoped the word "maybe" would be followed with an onslaught of other juicy details. But she'd stopped talking.

"Can you give me a name?" I prompted.

"I can give you *two* names. Right before Elias's death, he sent me a letter. He said Alexandra promised to keep some of the things he'd told her a secret. He also said he didn't trust her. He thought the day would come when she'd break her promise. Not at first, but one day. He asked me to do him a favor."

"What favor?"

"Inside the letter he sent to me were two additional letters. One addressed to Sandra Hamilton, the other to Paula Page. He said that once he died, I was to deliver the letters to them personally without opening them."

"Did you deliver them?" I asked.

"I didn't. I kept them."

It was like someone had just handed me the keys to a brand-new car.

"Where are the letters now? Can I see them?"

She shook her head. "I'm afraid not."

"Why not?"

"After Mrs. Weston left my house, I thought about what Elias had said all those years ago, about what he'd asked me to do. It occurred to me the purpose of her visit may not have been as it seemed. I felt she'd manipulated me, pressed me for details only I would know. Details she planned to include in her memoir to make it as scandalous as possible. I dug the letters out of an old file box the next day and hand-delivered them to Sandra and Paula."

"Did they wonder why you waited so long to deliver them?"

"I told them I'd happened upon the box he'd sent me from prison, and there they were."

"Did they accept the letters?"

"I thought they wouldn't, but both of them did."

"Is there any chance you read them first?" I asked.

She shook her head. "I didn't. Thought about it more than once. It would have been so easy to break the seal on the envelopes, read the letters, then deliver the letters and just say that was how they were sent to me. But those letters weren't meant for me. So I didn't read them."

"Did you say anything about Alexandra when you delivered the letters to Sandra and Paula?"

"I told them about her upcoming memoir."

"How did they react?"

"In a word—scared."

As the first unexpected shock settled in, Loretta unleashed a second, equally shocking bit of information.

"Personally I didn't care what Alexandra wrote in her tell-all book. There's nothing she can do now to hurt my family that she hasn't already done. I only asked her to leave the child out of it."

Was it possible? Had Loretta known the truth about Chelsea all this time?

"What child?"

"Elias's daughter. *My* granddaughter."

"Wait—you know about Chelsea?"

Loretta nodded.

It seemed everyone knew about Chelsea *except* Chelsea.

"How long have you known?" I asked.

"How do you think I learned of his sexual relations with Alexandra Weston? He had to tell me if he was going to tell me about the baby. There was no other way."

"What did you do after you found out?"

"Nothing."

"Why not?" I asked. "Weren't you interested in being part of her life?"

"Part of her life? If Alexandra had wanted me to be part of Chelsea's life, I would have been. She had her reasons, or her fears, I should say. I respected her need for discretion. I'd be lying if I said I hadn't imagined what it would be like to have a life with my granddaughter. But I thought it was for Chelsea's own good if I stayed away. I put her needs above my own. I suppose Alexandra did the same."

I didn't agree. "Alexandra should have told you about her. You're her family. You had every right to know."

"Why? Think about it. If the truth of who Chelsea really was got out, how do you think Chelsea would have been treated? Think about how much different her life would have been. I didn't want it to be ruined because of Elias. He'd already ruined the rest of my family."

I still didn't agree, but I saw her point. "I'm sorry for what you've been through, for your loss."

For the first time since I'd arrived, Loretta looked at me. *Really* looked at me. "What do you know about significant loss, Miss Jax? Has your heart been torn from you and yet you still continue to exist when you have little left to live for? Keep your sorry. I don't need it."

Finch glanced in my direction. I thought he might speak up. He didn't.

"I don't know what your loss feels like to you," I said. "I can't imagine. But you shouldn't assume you're the only one who has suffered."

"Did *your* son die cruelly in an electric chair? Did *your* friends shun you? Your family? Your neighbors? Your church? Was *your* husband forced to sell his company, the one he built from nothing? Did *you* walk into this very room and find your husband hanging from the beam you're sitting beneath at this very moment?"

Like a motorist passing the scene of an accident on the highway, I knew it was wrong to stare, but I did anyway. I couldn't help it. A minute earlier, I wouldn't have noticed the beam. Now it was etched into my mind forever. "I'm sorry. I didn't know about your husband."

"My husband Jeremiah could handle a lot things, but the one thing he couldn't was the loss of respect from everyone around him after Elias's crimes were revealed. People didn't look at us the same. We were judged, labeled bad parents, like we were to blame for Elias turning out the way he did. It was too much for him."

Too much?

Jeremiah still had a family who needed him. Family who didn't deserve to lose him too. A wife. Other children. How selfish he was to hang himself in his own home for his wife and his children to find. Some people might justify his actions. Not me.

"It must have been hard."

"What would you know about that?"

Plenty.

In that moment, the words I never seemed to find, the ones that stuck to my throat, always resisting the opportunity to find their way out, surged from me. "I lost my daughter."

"What do you mean you *lost* her?"

"I mean she's dead."

Loretta pressed a hand to her chest. "Why? What happened to her?"

"I happened. I made a mistake, and she lost her life because of it."

Even after I'd said it, I couldn't believe I had. I'd never discussed it before, and here I was revealing my deepest regret to a complete stranger. In an odd way, it was easier. I didn't know her. She didn't know me. I didn't care what she thought. And then I remembered

Finch. I'd become so caught up in the conversation, I forgot he was still there next to me, quietly taking it all in.

I braved my nerves to tilt my head just enough to look at him.

Now you see me.

The real me.

Raw.

Stripped down.

Broken.

Maybe now he'd understand why I lived my life the way I did. Always looking for the next rush, the next fix, the next thing to make the numb feeling inside me go away, to feel alive again, even if it was only for a fleeting moment.

As we sat there in silence, staring at each other, Loretta cut in. "What mistake did you make with your daughter? How is what happened to her on you?"

Before I could reply, Loretta's front door opened and shut, and a male voice said, "Mother?"

"In here," Loretta replied.

A man appearing to be in his mid-forties came around the corner, stopping abruptly when he realized Loretta wasn't alone. He seemed surprised. I doubted she received many visitors. He removed the outer jacket over his tailored gray suit, folding it in half before placing it over the edge of the sofa. His overall presence was polished and pristine, except for one oddity: a long, trimmed beard.

"This is my son Ethan," Loretta said.

Ethan sat next to his mother. "You didn't tell me anyone was stopping by today."

Loretta gestured at us with a hand. "I've only just met them. This is, umm, what did you say your names were again?"

"Joss and Finch," I said.

"Right. Joss and Finch."

Ethan snorted. "Finch? Is that a nickname or something? I mean, what kind of name is—"

"The kind you don't question," Finch replied.

Ethan stopped laughing. "Why are you here?"

"They were asking questions about Elias," Loretta said.

"Why?"

"I'm not sure."

Ethan's forehead wrinkled. "You let complete strangers in the house without even asking what they wanted? You can't do things like that."

"We're trying to find out about what happened to Alexandra Weston," I said.

"What does she have to do with my mother?" Ethan asked.

"I just had a few questions I thought she could answer, and she did. You have nothing to worry about."

"Oh, so you think you can say a few words, smooth things over, and I'm supposed to feel better now? I want you to leave. Now."

Finch stood. I remained seated.

"What do you do for a living, Ethan?" I asked.

"What business is it of yours?" he replied.

"My son has a wonderful job," Loretta beamed. "He owns a veterinary pharmaceutical company in Texas. Keeps him busy. Too busy, if you ask me. He only gets out here to see me a few times each year."

I faced Ethan. "Did you know Alexandra Weston was murdered this past week?"

He shook his head, like there was no need for me to state the obvious. "Uhh, *everyone* knows."

"The police are still working on finding her killer, but they're getting close."

He shrugged. "Good for them."

"Apparently there was a man following Chelsea the other day. He ran her off the road."

"A man following who?"

"You know," Loretta chimed in. "*Chelsea.*"

He looked at his mother like he'd do just about anything to keep her from talking. "Right. Chelsea."

"So you know she's your niece then?"

He laughed. "She's not my niece. I don't even know her."

"You may not, but it's still true."

"Yeah, well, as far as I'm concerned, she's not my blood."

With the environment turning hostile, I stood, walked with Finch to the door, the entire time thinking about the fact that Ethan had a job that granted him access to poison. We reached the car, and I turned to see Loretta arguing with her son on the porch. Ethan went back inside the house, slamming the door behind him. Loretta approached me. "A moment, Miss Jax, if you don't mind?"

"Sure," I said.

"I shouldn't have said what I did earlier. You're right. I don't know you. And you don't know me."

"No, you were right. I haven't dealt with what you've dealt with before. It's different for me."

"Pain is pain no matter how we choose to look at it. It's easy to think of our own loss and assume no one else's suffering is quite the same."

"We all face our own personal demons, don't we?" I said.

She nodded.

I gave her the name of my hotel in case she remembered anything else. She turned and walked back to the house, saying, "You take care of yourself. Don't spend your life wallowing in misery like I have. It's no way to live."

CHAPTER 43

"I HAVE A CONFESSION TO MAKE," FINCH SAID.

We were in the car headed back to the hotel. He'd been silent for almost ten minutes. Well, not completely silent, but humming. Humming while tapping his thumb on the steering wheel and staring out the window. Several miles back, we'd passed a billboard with a picture of Louis Armstrong playing a trumpet, and that was when the humming began.

"What's your confession?" I asked.

"At Elias's mother's house, you mentioned what happened to your daughter, and I ..."

Suddenly he couldn't finish his sentence. I knew he was stalling, having second thoughts about telling me.

"What's your confession, Finch?"

He pulled the car over, looked at me.

"What are you doing?" I asked. "Why are we stopping?"

"This isn't the kind of thing I just want to blurt out. It wouldn't feel right."

"Oh … kay."

He gripped the steering wheel like he was revving a throttle on a sports car. "I knew about your daughter already, about what happened to her, I mean."

"How long have you known?"

"Last year when you got hammered in that bar in Los Angeles … I can't remember what that place was called …"

"Tito's."

He nodded. "That's right. Tito's Bar. I'd been working for you for a while, and I'd never seen you drink more than a glass of wine or two, even when you were at a party. Then December rolls around and you're sitting alone at a table one night shooting vodka like it's water."

"Millions of people do it all the time, Finch."

"You don't. I figured whatever was going on with you, it must have been personal."

"Why?"

"I remember getting that drunk myself after finding out my wife destroyed our marriage."

"Still doesn't explain how you found out. Who told you?"

"No one. I'd never ask anyone else about your private life."

"How do you know then?"

"I got curious, looked it up on the Internet."

He hadn't just *looked it up*. He'd done a little digging. It wasn't hard to find, but it wasn't easy either. "If you knew, why ask me about it the other day?"

"I wanted you to feel like you could talk about it when you were ready. If you didn't, I'd wait and try again next year."

We drove several miles in silence before he spoke again. "I hope you're not upset with me," he said. "I should have told you. I know. I'm sorry."

"I'm not upset. You're right. *I* should have told *you*."

"No. I shouldn't have pried. It wasn't right."

"How much do you know?"

"Not much. I found one article on an online newspaper site. I read it, then decided I shouldn't have."

My cell phone buzzed, and the conversation with Finch was cut short. I spoke to Barbara Berry for several minutes, said I knew about Alexandra's memoir, asked if she wanted to admit she knew about the memoir too. She stuck to the same thing she'd said before, adding that since we'd last spoken she'd learned what Alexandra was really writing. Now that the funeral was over, Barbara was headed back to Chicago. We put a plan in motion for later that day, and she suggested meeting at the bed and breakfast where she was staying.

"Well, what did she say?" Finch asked after the call ended.

"That idea we discussed? She's game."

"We better get to the place she's staying then."

"The sooner the better."

I interlocked my hands behind my head and leaned back, knowing if the plan went well, it would lead me right to Alexandra's killer.

CHAPTER 44

FOLLOWING THE DIRECTIONS TO BARBARA'S ROOM ON the third floor of the house, I ascended the stairs, found a kid that looked like an employee standing in the hallway in front of her door, knocking. He seemed irritated. "Hello, ma'am, I'm here for your bags. Are you going to open the door so I can take them?"

The door didn't open. The employee reached his hand inside his pocket, took out a phone, and made a call. "Are you sure you sent me to the right room? No one's answering." There was a pause then he said, "I *am* standing in front of the presidential suite. Are you sure you have the time right?"

"Excuse me," I said. "How long have you been standing in front of Miss Berry's room?"

Without looking at me, he held a finger in the air, expecting me to wait until he finished his call. I lifted the phone out of his hand, pressed the end button.

He swung for the phone. Finch grabbed his wrist and said, "Don't touch her. Understand?"

"What are you ... let go of me!" the boy yelled.

"Answer the question," I said. "How long have you been waiting at Miss Berry's door?"

"Couple minutes maybe."

"How long ago did she call to ask for help with her bags?"

"She didn't call. She asked at breakfast this morning."

"Was breakfast the last time you saw Miss Berry?" I asked.

He nodded.

I handed his phone back. "How can I get inside her room?"

"Who are you?"

"A friend she was supposed to meet. Right now, actually."

"If she was supposed to meet you here, why was she leaving?"

"She was leaving after we spoke." I looked at Finch. "I don't have time for this. Go see if you can find a manager so we can get inside her room."

"I *knew* you weren't really here to meet her," the kid said. "Who are you?"

Finch started down the hall.

I looked at the kid, itching to smack the smug look off his face. "Did you hear about the murder of Alexandra Weston?"

He folded his arms in front of him. "Yeah. Who hasn't?"

"Miss Berry was Alexandra Weston's agent."

"So?"

"The man who killed Alexandra Weston hasn't been caught yet."

"Yeah, but what does that have to do with the lady staying here?"

I stepped in front of the kid, tried the knob on the door. It was unlocked. I pushed the door open and stepped inside. "Miss Berry, are you here?"

The kid came in after me. "You can't go in—"

I whipped around, slapped him across the face. Hard. "Shut. Up."

I searched the small, Victorian-style room for any sign of her. Finch called to me from downstairs. "Joss, get down here!"

I followed the sound of his voice down the stairs and into a small room that had been converted into a library. On the floor, in front of a pair of chairs, coffee had been spilled, and in front of that, still clutching the handle of the cup, was Barbara Berry's body.

I bent down, checked for a pulse.

A housekeeper entered the room and screamed, drawing the attention of everyone scattered around the house. As they gathered around, Finch stepped in front of Barbara, to keep the crowd at bay.

"What do you think?" Finch asked. "Can you tell from looking at her?"

"Is she dead?" one man asked.

"It appears she is."

"How do you know for sure?"

"I checked her pulse. There isn't one. I also checked her pupils. They appear to be dilated."

The housekeeper leaned down.

"Don't touch her," I said. "You could destroy the potential evidence on her body."

"How long has she been dead, do you think?" the housekeeper asked.

"Not long. We just spoke on the phone." I eyed the room. "Has anyone seen Barbara since breakfast?"

A man raised a finger. "I have."

"How long ago?"

"Let's see. She came downstairs when I was watching TV so I'd guess about two hours ago."

"Did she say anything?"

"Not a word."

"Do you know why she came downstairs?"

Another finger went up. "I'm Lori, the innkeeper here. She wanted to know if I had any chocolate croissants left. The ones we served at breakfast. I heated one up for her, and I thought she took it back to her room. Maybe she didn't."

I crouched down, scanned the floor, located the croissant, topside down, halfway across the room.

"Why didn't anyone notice she was in this room before now?"

"This room is hardly ever used."

"There's one other thing," Lori said. "I overheard Miss Berry talking on the phone a while ago. She invited someone to stop by before she headed to the airport. She said she had something in her possession she'd be willing to return for the right price."

"Did she say what she had?"

Lori nodded. "A flash drive."

CHAPTER 45

WHILE FINCH REMAINED DOWNSTAIRS WAITING FOR
the police, I returned to Barbara's room, this time focusing on the
room itself. Her luggage was open but empty, her clothes lined out
on the bed like she was preparing to arrange everything in her bags.
A laptop was on the nightstand. It was open, like she'd been using it
the last time she was in the room. I walked over, running my finger
along the keypad. The computer screen came to life, displaying a
typed message. I bent down and read it.

*The guilt I feel over Alex's death is constant, weighing on me more
and more with each passing day. It consumes me, so much so I can no
longer live with the evil truth of what I've done. I killed her, you see,
poisoned her drink in the same way I poisoned my own this morning. It
was me who ran Chelsea off the road. Me who broke into Alex's house,
making it look like a robbery. I needed the flash drive, and I was willing
to kill a dear friend to get it. Not for greed or for money, but to ensure her
memoir was never published. In the days since her death, nothing has
eased my sense of regret, and I make no excuses for what I've done.*

A light tapping sound came from the opposite side of Barbara's
bedroom door. I turned. A young girl of about twenty poked her head

in. Her hands were clasped together in front of her, like she was nervous and afraid.

"Yes?" I asked.

"A few minutes ago when you were talking to all of us downstairs, you asked if anyone saw anything suspicious. I did."

"Why didn't you say something before?"

"I don't know. I'm new here. I just got this job a week ago, and I don't want to cause any problems."

"A woman is dead," I said. "Why would it cause a problem if you told the truth?"

"What I saw might be nothing, but the more I think about it, the more I'm not sure."

"What did you see?"

"A woman coming out of Miss Berry's bedroom."

"What time?"

"Within the last hour."

"Are you sure it was a woman and not a man?"

She nodded.

"How old?" I asked.

"I don't know."

"You didn't get a good look at her?"

"I was coming around the corner, headed to the next room I had to clean. I assumed the woman was a friend of Miss Berry's, so I didn't think much of it. It all happened so fast, no more than five or ten seconds."

"Did you notice anything about her at all?"

"She wore a hat, and honestly, her hair didn't sit right."

"What kind of hat?"

"A beanie."

I pointed to my head. "Like mine?"

"It was longer and a charcoal color. It had a pom-pom on top."

"What do you mean her hair didn't look right?" I asked.

"What I mean to say is, it didn't look real."

I pressed her for the height, weight, and attire of the woman she saw. Again she struggled with her answers. She described the height and weight as average, and as far as clothing went, she could only remember the woman had on a large coat with a faux fur rim along the hood. Fake fur to match her alleged fake hair.

"Anything else?" I asked. "Did she talk to you?"

She shook her head. "She never even looked at me. She kept her head down, walked past me, and out the front door."

"Did you see where she went, or if she got into a car?"

"She didn't get into a vehicle. She walked down the street and went around the corner. I'm sorry. I feel like I'm not really helping."

"You're helping, more than you know," I said. "When the police get here, I want you to tell them everything you told me."

"The police *are* here," a male voice said.

Detective Murphy canvassed the room, then turned toward Blunt who was standing behind him. "Sounds like this girl has some useful information. Take her downstairs and see what she knows."

Blunt started to speak, but Murphy held up a hand. "Take her downstairs, Blunt. That will be all."

Both women left the room. Murphy walked over to the computer, bent down. "What's this then?"

"A typed suicide note."

He smiled, finding it amusing.

We exchanged information. I updated him on my visit with Elias's mother, and he told me Porter had dropped Alexandra's laptop by.

"We opened the password-protected book file," he said. "It was blank."

"The entire thing?" I asked.

"The entire thing, which means, it was wiped or transferred to another device, or wiped *and* transferred."

"What are you thinking?"

"My best guess? Someone transferred the file onto a flash drive. Could have been Alexandra Weston. Could have been someone else. Hard to say. Either way you look at it, someone's gone to great lengths to make sure that book doesn't get published." Murphy slid a pair of gloves on, riffled through the zippered parts of Barbara's bag. "I tried calling Miss Berry this morning. When she didn't answer, I called Pierce Glassman."

"Who's Pierce Glassman?"

"Alexandra's lawyer."

"Her lawyer?"

"Not her estate lawyer. The guy who looks over her publishing contracts. Alexandra has been a client of his since her first book. I heard he was a confidant. Someone she trusted implicitly."

I added her lawyer to the growing list of men she'd kept in her back pocket. "What did you find out from him?"

"Nothing. Seems no one is available for comment today. Called the guy three times already." Murphy laughed, but it was obvious he hadn't taken too kindly to being slighted.

"It's Saturday," I said. "He's not in the office."

Now on the third zippered pocket inside the suitcase, his eyes locked on something. Using a pen he'd pulled from his pocket, he lifted out a bag of white powder. Holding it up in front of him, he squinted his eyes, inspecting it. "What do you wanna bet this here is fluoroacetate, the same poison used to kill Alexandra Weston?"

"I'd say there's a slim chance it isn't."

He winked at me. "Convenient, isn't it?"

I nodded. A little *too* convenient.

CHAPTER 46

I FOUND PIERCE GLASSMAN STRETCHING AGAINST A gate in front of a house that looked like it was big enough to accommodate three families. Maybe four. His knee was bent, his hand palming a shoe grazing his left butt cheek. He looked to be in his mid-fifties and was short, five foot seven inches or so, but decked out in Nike from head to running shoe, his svelte body made up for every single inch of it and more. Body to body, he'd never measure up to Finch, no matter how hard he tried, but he was a pint-sized sight to behold nonetheless. I beheld for a solid minute before Finch caught me. He shook his head, pulled the car over, and I put the window down.

"Are you Pierce Glassman?" I asked.

Without turning, he replied, "Who's asking?"

"Joss Jax."

"Very funny. Try again."

"Turn around, Mr. Glassman."

He turned and eyed me then Finch, unfazed. "What can I do for you, Joss?"

"Detective Murphy has been calling you all morning. You haven't returned his call."

"I will later, when I have time."

"You're finished with your run, aren't you? Looks like you have time right now."

"I need a shower. Then I have some paperwork to go over. Then I have a dinner date."

"Suit yourself. If you don't return his call, he'll be coming over later."

"I won't be here."

"Barbara Berry is dead," I said.

"When?"

"This morning."

"How?"

"Killed herself."

"How?"

"Poison."

He raised a brow. "Forgive me if I have a hard time believing she'd off herself. Are you certain?"

"She left a suicide note."

His eyes expanded significantly, but he maintained his nonchalant, unaffected attitude. "Saying what, exactly?"

"Saying she's responsible for the death of Alexandra Weston."

"You're joking, right? You must be."

"No joke, Mr. Glassman."

"What reason did Barb give for killing Alex?"

"She killed her to keep Alexandra's memoir from being published."

"What?"

Pulling his shirt up, he wiped his face with it, then approached the car. When he leaned down and stuck his head through the window, the car filled with an unsavory stench of sweat and body odor. Maybe he was trying to make me go away. I wasn't going anywhere.

"What do you know about Alexandra Weston's memoir?"

He shook his head. "Can't tell you that."

"The book has gone missing from Alexandra's computer. The police have her laptop. The file is there, but the manuscript is gone."

"What do you mean *gone*?"

"I mean someone either erased it, or transferred it to a flash drive and then erased it. You wouldn't happen to have a copy or know where I can get one?"

"I don't read her books. I just negotiate the contracts. I'm not a storage facility."

"I didn't ask if you read it or not," I said.

"Then what *are* you asking?"

"Did she ever talk to you about the contents of the book?"

"No."

"Did she ever express concern about anyone being upset with her over what she wrote in the book?"

His head indicated *no*, but his eyes said *yes*.

"Did someone threaten her?" I asked.

He didn't reply.

"Someone did. Who? I already know about Paula Page. Anyone else I need to add to the list?"

"Like I said, I don't know. You're wasting your time and mine. I can't help you."

He stood up and smacked the hood of the car with his fist like he was giving us permission to drive away. Of course, we didn't.

"It just seems odd," I persisted. "Barbara has been Alexandra's agent for years. To my knowledge, they've never quarreled, never had a falling out, and had nothing but respect for each other. And now I'm supposed to believe this crazy scenario where Barbara kills Alexandra and then herself?"

The attorney sighed. "I don't know what the hell is going on here, but all I'll say is this: Barb wouldn't have stopped the book deal. She had no reason to. Even if the contents within the book were scathing, Barb still would have pushed to publish it. As far as

Alex goes, she offended a handful of people over the years."

"Just give me a name," I said. "One name. I'm sure someone comes to mind. If you had to name one person who wanted Alexandra dead, who would it be?"

"I've said more than I wanted to already."

"You haven't said anything."

"Good meeting you, Joss." He turned and walked away, but shouted over his shoulder, "Barb didn't kill Alex, by the way."

"I know she didn't," I yelled.

I know.

CHAPTER 47

January 10, 1990

ELIAS PRATT STOOD TALL AND STRAIGHT, HANDS CLASPED around the metal bars of his cell, reflecting on what would become the last moments of his life. Earlier in the day, he'd been told the execution team, the "strap-down people" as they were called, had completed their series of pre-death rehearsals. The oak chair known as Gruesome Gertie had been tested on several occasions by a man similar to Elias's height and weight. The man had sat in the chair, checked the straps, ensured the seat was sturdy—solid enough to perform its duty that night without fail.

What sparse belongings Elias had were boxed up and labeled for shipment to his mother. His head had been shaved, and an adult diaper secured, hidden beneath his pants.

Whether or not he feared what was about to come next, it didn't matter; the hour was at hand. Now, moments away from being escorted to the execution chamber, he felt no differently than he had the night he'd crouched over Sandra Hamilton's body, waiting to be picked up by the police. It was a kind of numb resignation. The very same resignation he'd felt his entire life. Admitting it to himself now, he felt lighter, like a bar of truth had been lifted. Life. Death. It didn't matter. Aging only put off the inevitable death all people experienced in the end. Only his end would have nothing to do with old age.

During his time in prison, Elias had tried reaching out to Sandra through letters. He wanted to explain what happened the night she found her parents on the kitchen floor, to make her understand the motive behind their murders, behind why both of her parents died by his own hand. Contrary to his other murders, theirs had nothing to do with a robbery or because of a desire to kill. But he imagined she knew already.

He'd loved her.

At least, he'd thought he loved her at the time.

Now he was certain his skewed idea of love was much different than the feelings most men and women had for each other.

Still, he'd been smitten ever since the first time he saw her step out of Toby Fink's car at the drive-in, ratted hair pulled back in a pink and white polka-dot scrunchy, acid-washed jeans so tight they looked like they were painted on. Elias wanted to touch her, to be near her, to learn everything about her. And he had.

The good.

The bad.

The secret so revolting his blood sizzled like water boiling over on a stove when he learned it.

His thoughts turned to Paula. If he had been capable of love, true love, he now knew it would have been for her. While plain and simple, the kind of girl most men never gave a second glance at, she was more devoted to him than any woman had ever been. So devoted, she had killed because of her love for him. He only wished he'd realized his true feelings for her before he'd crouched over Sandra, sacrificing his life for hers when he could have turned and fled. Fled and never looked back. Now he realized why Paula did what she did afterward, and why she told everyone she'd been raped. She'd killed for him, and still, he'd given up his life over Sandra.

Two officers approached Elias's cell. The taller one muttered, "It's time." He didn't look Elias in the eye when he said it. The other officer shouted for Elias's cell to be opened. As the cell gate parted in front of him, Elias couldn't help but wish it could remain shut.

Officers positioned themselves on both sides. He was then escorted into a room built with cinderblocks. The blocks were painted a dingy shade of white, which perfectly matched the tone of the room and what it was used for sometimes. Gruesome Gertie was in the center of the room, unoccupied and alone, her appearance so frightening he took two steps back when he saw her. The shorter of the two guards shoved him forward, and in one swift, surreal moment, Elias was stuffed into the chair. In seconds the leather straps were secured. One under the chin. One across the chest. One around his waist. Two over his wrists and elbows. A tight mask was positioned on his head, waiting to be pulled over his face when the time was right.

The warden, coroner, and physician were all in place, eyes shiny, seeming almost too eager for the show to begin. Through the two-way glass in front of him, he scanned left to right, recognizing many faces in attendance. There were a few witnesses from prior victims' families, at least two members of the news media, his mother, and one of his brothers.

No Sandra and no Paula—only a faithful Alexa Weston sitting in the middle of the second row. Her face was stern, emotionless. In the company of everyone else, Elias figured she had no choice but to be impartial. To the world, she was supposed to see him the way they all did, as nothing more than a ruthless killer. He supposed it was true. No matter what spin she spun in her book to make him seem humane, he wasn't. He smiled, recalling the past, knowing how proficiently he'd worked her over. He was sure she loved him, in her way, and she probably thought he felt the same, even though he didn't.

Sitting here now, watching her smooth a hand over her abdomen, over *his* baby, his unborn seed, he was filled with satisfaction.

My legacy will live on.

A man placed a microphone in front of Elias's face. "Do you have a final statement?"

He leaned forward, eyed Alexa for the last time, and spoke the words of investigative journalist I.F. Stone. "Every emancipation has in it the seeds of a new slavery, and every truth easily becomes a lie."

The headpiece was slipped over his face, and as the first round of electrical currents was administered and his body strained against the straps, he laughed and laughed and laughed, knowing no witness in the room, save one, would ever understand the last thing he had to say.

CHAPTER 48

November 29, 2015
Alexandra Weston

SITTING IN A LIVING ROOM FAR SMALLER THAN THE ONE she'd sat in many years earlier, Alexandra did what she didn't do best. She waited. Stared at Paula Page. Paula stared at the floor. Alexandra wanted to move things along, but knew she couldn't. Not yet. First she needed to allow ample time for Paula to absorb what she'd just said.

A minute ticked by.

Then two.

Paula, it seemed, was too rattled to speak.

Not that Alexandra blamed her.

Writing a "where are they now" version of the most famous criminals Alexandra had interviewed over her thirty-five-year career was something she had no interest doing. The idea was good, and she had no doubt the book would sell well. The problem was, it didn't fit into her plans to publish her memoir and retire. With this project taking up so much of her time, her memoir would have to wait until the following year.

Since publishing Elias's story twenty-five years earlier, Alexandra had come to see him in a different light. No longer young and naïve like she was when she wrote about him the first time, she could now see how he'd manipulated her, clouded her mind into writing the story *he* wanted her to tell. She regretted it. No man had ever managed that before, and no man since. Even now, she didn't know how she had been so blind.

The opportunity to fix past mistakes was an opportunity at redemption. It wouldn't be jaded or muddled with confused emotion. It would be filled with only one thing: truth. Part of that truth was sitting across from her now.

At long last, Paula's mouth opened, and what followed was exactly what Alexandra expected. "What are you going to do with the information you know about me?"

"Nothing yet."

"What do you mean *yet*? What do you want to keep quiet?"

"I don't want anything," Alexandra said.

"Then why are you telling me?"

"I thought you should know."

"How do you think it's going to look when everyone finds out you knew I shot Sandra and you kept it to yourself?"

Alexandra crossed one leg over the other. "How stupid do you think I am? I'm not going to say I found out all those years ago. I'm going to say I only recently discovered it."

"Then I'll say you always knew."

Alexandra bobbed her shoulders up and down. "Do whatever you like. No one will believe you over me."

"Look around, Mrs. Weston. I've lost everything. My husband. My home. Thanks to you, he divorced me after finding out I lied about being raped. Imagine how it felt to lose the life I had and then find out you left it out of the book anyway. I don't understand why you did it."

"I made Elias a promise, and I shouldn't have."

"How is your promise any different now than it was then?"

"It isn't. I just see things clearly now. And the truth is I don't care what you think or what you want or what will happen to you when my book is released. I care that he made a fool of me, and now I intend to set it right."

"You're a bitch."

Alexandra stood, slung her handbag over her shoulder, patted Paula on the shoulder, and laughed. "Good for you! Get it off your chest. Feels good, doesn't it, to say what you wanted to say since the moment I walked in here? I like your spirit."

Alexandra headed for the door.

"We're not done talking."

Alexandra turned. "Oh yes, we are."

"If I'm going down, she is too."

Interest piqued, Alexandra asked, "Who's *she*?"

"Sit back down, Mrs. Weston. There's something you should know about Sandra Hamilton."

CHAPTER 49

Present Day

ON THE TABLE INSIDE MY HOTEL ROOM I SPIED A WHITE envelope with my name on it propped against a vase on the desk. I dialed the receptionist and was told the envelope had been left for me an hour earlier. I opened it, unfolded the pages inside. The first page contained a letter handwritten in cursive ink.

This mess with Alexandra Weston is something I didn't want my family to be caught up in. Not again. But as the news came on this evening and I learned of Barbara Berry's death, I wondered who else might be in danger. I thought about Chelsea, and I thought about you, so determined to find answers, I imagine you'll never stop until you have them. If something happened to Elias's daughter, I don't think I could forgive myself. So yes, the truth is I read Elias's letters to Sandra and Paula. Then I sealed them in a different envelope and gave them to them, just like I said I did. After Alexandra's visit, I was angry. I didn't like the idea of her writing another book, dragging out the past. It was clear to me that the affection she'd once had for Elias had changed, and I believed she was out to stir up trouble for my family again.

In Elias's letters to both women, he was kind and apologetic. I wish I could say that's all they were, but they were much more. Elias told Paula that Alexandra was pregnant with his baby. He asked Paula to kill Alexandra after the baby was born, and raise the baby as her own. He told her where he'd hidden all the items he'd stolen from all the robberies and said she'd have enough money to take the baby and run away.

So many years had come and gone, I didn't think it would matter whether I gave the letter to Paula anymore. Chelsea's a grown woman. She wouldn't get taken now. Paula has moved on with her life. As for his request to end Alexandra's life, I figured Paula would have a good laugh at Elias's expense for even thinking she'd consider it.

As I write this now, I have to wonder whether I was wrong. As for what Elias said to Sandra, well, I suggest you talk to her about that yourself. You seem like a good person, Miss Jax. In light of recent events, I'd encourage you to take precautions and not to see either woman alone. Take that beautiful boy with you.

Good luck.

Loretta Pratt

CHAPTER 50

TWO HOURS LATER, I SAT IN THE LOBBY OF MY HOTEL across from two disgruntled women.

"Thank you both for meeting me tonight," I said.

Paula looked at Sandra then at me. "You never said *she'd* be here. I shouldn't have agreed to this."

"You agreed because I told you I knew about the letters Elias wrote you," I said. "I wasn't aware you two had a problem with each other."

Dressed in a loose-fitting tank top in the middle of winter, jeans, and a cheap pair of flip-flops, Sandra looked like she could be bought for a dollar and change if the right guy was interested. She slouched in her seat, kicked her feet over the top of the table, and said, "We don't have a problem with each other. Why would we?"

Paula rolled her eyes. Clearly one of them didn't agree. "Why are we here? What do you want?"

"I'll get straight to it. Which one of you killed Alexandra Weston and Barbara Berry?"

Paula shot out of her chair, stuck a flattened hand in my direction. "Whoa, wait a minute. I didn't come here to be accused of anything, especially something I didn't do."

Finch, who was sitting two tables away, leaned around the book he was pretending to read and said, "Sit down, Paula."

She crossed her arms in front of her. "Who the hell are you?"

"Do what he says," I said.

She remained standing, defiant, glancing around, assessing all possible exits.

"Now," I said.

Sandra laughed in amusement, remained seated.

Paula lowered herself back into her seat. "I didn't kill anyone."

"I know what was in your letter," I said.

"You're full of it. You couldn't possibly know. Elias is dead, and the letter was sealed when it was given to me."

"What if I told you the letter was read and put into a different envelope before it was delivered to you, so it appeared like it hadn't been opened?"

"I still say you're bluffing. If you knew what it said, you wouldn't play games. You'd just tell me."

Sandra perked up, curious to hear my answer.

"For starters, Elias's mother was supposed to give you the letter right after Elias died, and she didn't," I said.

"She said she only recently went through the box," Paula said.

"Don't you find it a little too convenient that right after Alexandra Weston told Loretta she was writing a memoir that included a chapter on her son that Loretta finally decided to deliver the letters?"

"What are you saying—the three of us conspired to kill Alexandra to keep her from releasing the book?"

"It's possible," I said.

"I don't know Loretta, and I don't know Sandra either. We didn't meet up together, and we didn't make any plans. There's nothing going on here. Nothing, mmm … kay?"

"On the other hand, Alexandra was poisoned," I said, "which could have easily been a one-person job."

"Well, I didn't do it," Paula said.

"I didn't do it either," Sandra said. "Can't say I'm sorry she's dead though."

"Why?" I asked.

"She tried to scare me, told me she was writing about my family in her memoir."

"And it didn't upset you?"

Sandra brushed a hand through the air. "I mean, yeah, I guess. It doesn't affect me though. I don't care what other people think. I am who I am. Period."

I shifted the focus back to Paula. "Elias asked you to kill Alexandra in his letter. He wanted you to kidnap the baby, his baby, and raise her yourself."

Sandra sat straight up in her chair, grinning like she was witnessing a riveting scene in a movie. "He wanted you to kill Alexandra Weston and take her baby? Wow. That's messed up."

"Not now," Paula said. "Twenty-five years ago."

"Were you surprised when you read what he wanted you to do?" I asked.

"He was crazy to think I'd do it," Paula said. "But then, this is Elias we're talking about. He *was* crazy. And I was too stupid to notice. I thought I knew him. I worshipped him. The guy I fell in love with wasn't real, just a man I created in my mind."

"He created what he wanted you to see. He did the same thing to Alexandra, and as smart as she was, she fell for it too."

"Why take her baby though?" Paula asked. "And why ask me to keep it? I don't get it."

"He must have asked you because he thought you would do it. What I don't understand is … why?"

"Because I—" Paula stopped and her eyes flitted around the room.

"Because you what?" Sandra asked. "What's your deal? Just say what you need to say."

Tiny sweat beads gathered in the creases on Paula's forehead. She wiped her brow with her hand, tried to act normal. I looked at Finch. He saw it too. We all did.

With all of us focusing on Paula, I asked the question that had been on my mind since I learned about her letter. "Why would he ask you to kill for him?"

Instead of looking at me, she looked at Sandra. "I don't know."

"He must have thought you were capable of it. What would make him think that?"

She glanced at Sandra again.

I was missing something. Something big.

"Sandra," I said. "What was in *your* letter?"

"A bunch of bullshit."

"Meaning?"

"He didn't shoot me," Sandra said.

"What?"

"He said the night my parents were killed, he didn't shoot me."

"How's that possible? If he didn't shoot you, who did? And if someone else shot you, was he trying to say he had an accomplice?"

"Who knows?"

I turned again to Paula. "What do you know that you're not saying?"

"Nothing."

"You were his girlfriend, Paula. You know something. I can tell. We *all* can."

Paula gripped the corner of the side table next to her, like if she didn't grab hold of something she'd slide off her chair. In a hushed voice, she said, "I'm sorry. It was a long time ago."

"Sorry for what?" I asked.

She faced Sandra. "Sorry for shooting you, Sandra."

CHAPTER 51

IN HINDSIGHT, THE LOBBY OF MY HOTEL MAY NOT HAVE been the best place for me to meet Sandra and Paula, but it served a purpose I needed it to serve. Armed with the news Paula was responsible for shooting her the night her parents died, Sandra dove from her chair and went straight for the jugular, turning the hotel lobby into a boxing arena featuring one seriously furious, and possibly high, middle-aged chick. Sandra tackled Paula to the ground, knocking over Paula's chair with Paula still in it, then straddling her on the floor. Hands gripped around Paula's neck, Sandra made good use of every foul word in her extensive arsenal.

A curious crowd gathered, eyes wide, more interested in watching the girl-on-girl display than breaking it up. As Paula gasped for the smallest pocket of air, her face reddened to various shades. Finch reached down, grabbed a fistful of the back of Sandra's shirt. He yanked her off Paula, pushing her back into a chair. He commanded she stay there.

For the moment, she listened.

"Catch your breath, and get a grip," Finch said. "But your ass stays in that chair." He turned to the growing crowd. "This is private business. Get lost."

I gazed across the mass of people still unwilling to separate, studying their faces before kneeling next to Paula. She was half-coughing, half-gagging, and one-hundred-percent struggling to breathe. Her neck was swollen and red with visible imprints of where Sandra's fingers had just been. I did my best to calm her down, settle her breathing. When she'd swallowed enough air to form words again, she turned her head toward Sandra, and yelled, "I said I was sorry!"

Sandra rolled her eyes. "Sorry? Sorry doesn't cut it. You shot me! I could have died!"

"You *should* have died, but you didn't. Elias plugged the bullet hole in your chest. *That's* why you're still alive."

Sandra shook her head. "What are you talking about?"

"Don't you remember? He took his mask off, and you looked at him right before you passed out."

"When I came to, it was all a blur. I remember seeing his hands when they cuffed him. They were red and bloody, and I didn't know why."

"Now you know. He saved your life. A life you've wasted."

"What do *you* know about my life?"

"A lot more than you think. One of my friends is a friend of yours. I hear things. Even when I don't want to, and believe me, I don't."

"What about my parents?" Sandra asked. "Did you shoot them too? Leave Elias to take the blame for two murders that weren't his?"

"I didn't have anything to do with your mother and your stepdad. He killed them. And you know why he did it."

"No, I don't."

"Sure you do. Your mother knew your stepdad was sexually abusing you, and she did nothing to stop it."

Sandra's eyes narrowed. "How do *you* know about that?"

"After I shot you, he told me."

The conversation had taken a personal turn, with both women speaking to each other like they'd forgotten they were in a public place. The way Sandra dressed, the way she talked, fast and loose—it all made sense now.

"Elias didn't even know me," Sandra said. "Not really. Why would he risk everything for me? I don't get it."

"He knew your story."

"How? I never even met the guy."

"You did. You just didn't know it. Elias saw you out one night. He overheard you telling a friend all about your situation at home. You were crying to her, admitting what your stepdad had done. Your friend told you to tell your mom and you said you had. Your mom didn't believe you. She chose to ignore your accusations and pretend it wasn't happening."

"It still doesn't explain why you shot me," Sandra said.

"We were going to run away and get married, and then he saw you. Sad, considering you never noticed him. Once he knew your story, he obsessed over you. I became nothing to him. I was jealous. I'm not a mean-spirited person."

Sandra snorted a laugh. "Yeah, uhh, right."

"I mean it. I'm really not. I was just young and stupid and in love with the wrong guy."

Sandra laughed. "Save it. I don't need your excuses. I don't care."

"If you don't care, why choke me?"

"You deserved it." Sandra pulled her tank top down, exposing a faded scar on the front of her chest. "Every day for the last twenty-five years, I get out of the shower, see this scar, and am reminded of that night."

I crossed my arms in front of me, stepped forward. "You both have cleared up a lot of past history, but it still doesn't solve Alexandra's and Barbara's murders."

"I already told you, I didn't do it," Paula said.

Sandra looked at Finch like she didn't dare make a move without his permission. "Same. Can we go now?"

"Soon," Finch said.

"Alexandra was going to include a chapter about Elias in her memoir and, more than likely, expose both of your secrets," I said.

"Paula, my guess is Alexandra found out you shot Sandra somehow. What I don't understand is why wouldn't Alexandra put it in the original book she wrote about him then?"

None of us had a good answer for this, and with Elias *and* Alexandra dead, odds were it wouldn't change. "Paula, when did Alexandra tell you she knew you shot Sandra?"

"A couple months back. She said she wanted to give me a chance to tell my side of the story. I refused. She was upset I didn't give her what she wanted, and she left."

"And you didn't have any contact with her again?"

"Not until Elias's mother showed up with the old letter Elias had written. I knew then I had a way to stop her. I knew her kid wasn't her husband's. I called Alexandra, threatened to expose her if she exposed me."

"She came to my house too," Sandra said. "She told me she knew about my situation with my stepdad. I didn't have the trump card Paula had. My letter from Elias was a simple apology. He was proud he'd killed my parents. He thought I'd be happy. Free. When I cried over them the night they were killed, he didn't understand why. Were they bad parents? Maybe. But they were my only family."

Hearing her story, Paula's eyes welled with tears.

"Don't get all weepy on me," Sandra said. "I just tried to take you out."

"You were right though. I deserved it."

Paula stuck a hand out toward Sandra. "Truce?"

Sandra smacked it away. "Get your truce the hell away from me. We're not friends. We'll never be friends."

"I asked both of you to bring the letters tonight," I said. "I'd like to see them."

"What are you planning to do with them?" Paula asked.

"I don't know yet. For now, I'd just like to read them."

The letters were handed over. I read them, handed them to Finch to read too. I had a gift for forgetting things. Anything he read was committed to memory.

The letters were just as Sandra and Paula said. Nothing more. I handed them back. "If you can agree not to attack each other, I have one final question for you, Paula, and then we're done. What did you do with the leverage you had about Alexandra's daughter?"

"Nothing. I threatened her, said if she published the information about me, I'd destroy her life. And by destroy, I *don't* mean kill. I'd tell everyone about the child she had with Elias, but first, I'd tell her daughter myself. Part of me thought I'd tell her anyway. The girl deserves to know the truth."

"How did she respond?" I asked.

"Not in the way I expected. The only thing she said was, 'You'll never get anywhere near my daughter, and even if you do, by then it will be too late.'"

CHAPTER 52

Alexandra Weston
December 5, 2015

ALEXANDRA SAT ON THE SOFA, JAW CLENCHED, WATCHING the tears flow down her daughter's cheeks. It wasn't easy telling Chelsea the man she'd called Dad all her life wasn't really her father, but life wasn't easy. Chelsea was getting married soon, moving out, living on her own. It was time she learned to deal with challenges like a grown-up.

Though Alexandra had given up smoking a decade before, the past few weeks had been grueling. So now, as nothing she could say offered Chelsea the degree of solace she was looking for, Alexandra reached for the matte-black pack of Wills Insignia cigarettes beside her, ready to indulge in a few relaxing puffs. "Really, Chelsea, you need to calm down. It's hard for me to talk to you when you're like this."

"Calm down? Are you kidding me? How am I going to tell my fiancé? How am I going to tell his parents? They'll never understand. They'll never allow him to marry me after they find out."

Alexandra leaned back, flicked the metal on the side of her lighter, and lit up. She took a long drag, tried to keep calm as Chelsea's anger flared.

"So what, you're done talking to me now?" Chelsea asked. "You think you can tell me something like this, and then move on?"

"I said what I had to say. I told you the truth. I'm not sure what else you need from me."

"I *need* answers! How's it even possible that man … that horrible, disgusting man was my real father?"

The single infraction, the one, scandalous transgression between Alexandra and Elias, had lasted less than two minutes. Two short, premature ejaculatory minutes and poof, she was knocked up with his baby. Explaining how it came to occur or why it occurred was pointless. "What matters is it happened, and I felt you were old enough to hear it. Apparently, I was mistaken."

"Old enough? You're lying. I know how you work, Mother. You never would have told me if you didn't have to, so why are you?"

Alexandra curved her body forward, dipping the cigarette into a square metal tray on the coffee table. "You're right. I spent my life trying to forget it, trying to give you a good life, trying to keep it contained."

"How did it get out?"

"I suspect Elias's mother had something to do with it," Alexandra said. "When I visited with her recently, I told her I was writing a memoir about my life."

"Why did you tell her about me? She didn't need to know."

"I've asked myself the same question. I'm not sure why I did it. You're grown now. The woman looked like whatever life was left in her was trickling out. Surprise was on me though. She knew about you already. She'd always known. Before Elias died, he told her."

"How did *he* know?"

"I told him."

"Wait … what about Dad? Does he know?"

Alexandra nodded. "Your father found out when you were a

little girl. I hadn't planned on telling him either. He happened upon some information, and there was no denying it. I may not love him, and he may not love me, but he loves you, and I love you. Nothing else matters."

"Why didn't he tell me? Dad never keeps things from me."

"He had his reasons."

Chelsea snatched her phone off the sofa cushion. "This isn't fair! I'm calling him. I'm calling him right now!"

"Put the phone down, Chelsea."

"No!"

"Put the phone down. Your father doesn't know I've talked to you about this yet."

"Why, Mother? Why didn't he tell me?"

"Because I threatened him. I told him if he did I would divorce him and fight for full custody. He would have never seen you again."

Thinking the effort she'd gone to all these years to shield Chelsea from the truth would mean something to her daughter, she expected understanding and appreciation. Instead, it backfired.

"What's *wrong* with you?!"

"What's wrong with *me*?" Alexandra asked. "Nothing is wrong with me. I protected you by keeping the secret. I kept it from you *because* I love you. You're the one who's being irrational now. This isn't just about *you*. This doesn't just affect *you*. It affects me too. You think I wanted this to happen? You think I wanted it to come out? I'm not proud of it. If I had my way, it would stay buried forever."

"Stop saying you protected me! You only protected yourself. It's what you always do. You've ruined my life." Chelsea snatched a figurine of a bird off the coffee table and threw it across the room. It smashed to pieces against the wall.

"That's quite enough," Alexandra said. "Do you understand?"

"I hate you for this!"

Alexandra raised a hand, striking Chelsea across the face. The slap was firm and hard, echoing throughout the room. "I could have had an abortion and been done with it. Believe me, I thought about it multiple times."

Chelsea stood. Running from the room, she said, "You should have had an abortion. I wish you did!"

CHAPTER 53

Chelsea Wells
Five Minutes Later
ENRAGED, CHELSEA RAN UPSTAIRS, LOCKING HERSELF inside her room. She stared into the mirror, horrified to see the imprint of her mother's hand on her face. Days like today she hated her. Really, really hated her.

It was around age nine when Chelsea had first felt abandoned by her mother. While other girls whined about their own mothers being "too involved" in their lives, Chelsea was jealous of the relationships they all had. Her friends didn't know how lucky they were. Her mother may have been around a majority of the time, but she wasn't really *there*, not in the way a mother was supposed to be.

Their relationship was routine. Her mother asked if she had a good day at school. Chelsea said yes. Her mother smiled, and then returned to her office where she buried herself in whatever book project she was working on. Over time, Chelsea felt alone. If it hadn't been for the love of her father, a man who wasn't even her own flesh and blood, she wouldn't have had any parental support in her life.

The neglect from her mother over the years had left a gaping hole inside her, a void that wasn't filled until the day she met Bradley Claiborne. If his parents ever found out who her real father was, she knew they wouldn't approve of the marriage, and their approval had always been important to Bradley. She leaned back on the bed, weighing all possible outcomes.

They would marry just like they planned, and her mother's secret would stay buried.

She'd finally found real happiness, and nothing was getting in the way.

CHAPTER 54

Present Day

THE SHOT RANG OUT WITH A LOUD CRACK, THE BULLET whizzing by me in surreal slow motion. It was a crap shot fired with a pistol loosely gripped inside a shaky hand, and yet, it still connected with Finch's chest. Undeterred and unwilling to allow something so small to take him down, Finch shoved me behind him and lunged forward, swiping at the gun.

The gun cracked again.

This time, Finch went down.

I screamed.

Using the gun like it was an extension of his hand, Porter shifted his body, aimed at me. "Don't even think about moving."

Red liquid soiled Finch's shirt. I dropped to his side, my emotions clouding the rational thought I needed in this moment.

"I said don't move!" Porter barked. "On your feet. Get up. Now!"

I was unarmed and outmatched, but not outwitted.

"Fuck off!" I replied.

"I'll shoot you. I'll shoot you right now."

"No you won't. When I walked through your door, I told you I had something you needed. Something you'll never get if I'm not alive to give it to you."

"Where is it?!"

I turned toward Finch. "Don't move. Please. Stay where you are. I'm sorry. I'm so sorry."

He coughed through his words. "No … I'm sorry … I should have done a better job of protecting you."

"It's going to be okay," I said. "Hang on for me, okay? Just hang on."

"Save your breath, kid," Porter said. "Stand up, Joss. Move away from him."

I stood. I didn't step away. "I thought you said you were moving out of Alexandra's house? And yet, here you are, in your pajamas no less. Did you pop back for one last sleepover, or were those boxes I saw the other day all a part of the lie?"

No reply.

"Where's Chelsea?" I asked.

"She's eloping with Bradley, then taking an extended honeymoon. She won't return for a month, at least. When did you know it was me?"

"I saw you earlier tonight at the hotel, standing behind the crowd, watching the fight between Paula and Sandra. Your fake beard and hat was a mediocre disguise; I could tell it was you."

"You think you're such a clever girl, don't you? I knew the moment you recognized me tonight. Your eyes doubled in size. You looked nervous. I *knew* you'd come for me tonight. And, as you can see, I was fully prepared for you to come through that door."

"I'm a lot more clever than you think."

"You? You spent the entire week running in circles when the person you were searching for was in front of you all along."

"Did I really? Are you certain what you're saying is true?"

There it was. My confidence. His fear.

I'd rattled him.

"I see you switched from poison to a classic, old-fashioned gun," I said.

He shrugged. "You two gave me no choice. I offered you a drink the other day. You accepted. Your sidekick refused. I realized if I needed to kill you both, poison wasn't the answer. I had to get through him to get to you. A pistol provided the best solution."

"Would you like to know something? For days I've been thinking about something Roland Sinclair said to me after Alexandra's funeral."

"Yeah? What's that?"

"He didn't believe you were capable of killing Alexandra," I said.

"He was jealous. I had her—*really* had her. The ball *and* the chain. He didn't."

"Jealousy had nothing to do with his reasoning. Besides, if we're talking about who had her heart, I'd say Roland wins that category. He said you weren't smart enough to pull off her murder. At the time, I disagreed. Anyone is capable of murder, even the simpleminded ones like you. I am curious about one thing though. Why poison?"

"It was the easiest method."

To administer, yes. To acquire, no.

"Where did you get it?" I asked.

"I paid someone to get it for me. Money will get you anything these days."

"How did you get it into Alexandra's coffee?"

"It doesn't matter now, does it? She's dead."

"How much did you give her?"

He laughed. "Enough to kill her."

"That's not what I asked."

He pulled the hammer back, aimed, prepared to fire. "What do you have that I need?"

"Alexandra's flash drive, the one with her memoir on it."

He dug into his pants pocket, pulled out a small piece of plastic. "You mean *this* flash drive?"

I reached into my own pocket, pulling an identical storage device. "No, I mean *this* flash drive."

He looked at mine, then looked at his. They were both the same. "No. No. You're lying."

"If you truly believe you have the right one, try it out."

"Don't move." Keeping the gun on me, he sidestepped to the desk, stuck the flash drive into the portal in the desktop computer. Waited. "It's blank. There's nothing here. Where is it?"

I shook my hand back and forth. "I told you. It's right here."

"Give it to me!"

"The other night when someone broke into your house, you assumed it was Barbara Berry," I said. "It wasn't. It was me. I'm guessing that's why you killed her—to get what you thought she had. Only she didn't have it. I did."

Palms sweaty, he gazed once more at the plastic stick in his hand. "I don't understand. This came from Barbara's purse."

"When did you take it from Barbara's purse? Earlier today when you killed her?"

He stuck out his hand. "Toss it to me right now. You're dead anyway."

I tossed it over. Fearing he would shoot now that he had what he wanted, I said, "You might want to check it first."

He yanked out the other stick, stuck in the one I'd thrown to him. "There's nothing on this one either!"

Shaken, he struggled to make sense of what was happening, "It must have been the wrong … no, it couldn't be. She said it was the same one. She was sure it was the same one. If these are both the wrong one, then …"

Realization.

"Barbara asked to see me today," I said. "She was dead by the time I arrived. One of the employees said she saw a woman leaving Barbara's room. Not you, Porter. Not a man. A woman. A young woman. Chelsea. And you just confirmed it when you said *she* told you the book was all there on the flash drive."

He swallowed hard with the realization that the night wasn't going as planned. "Doesn't matter. They'll find no trace of Chelsea in Barbara's room. It's like I said before, Chelsea's gone now. It's too late."

"Tonight, when I saw you in the crowd, you saw what you wanted to see, just like you're seeing what I want you to see now."

"Enough! You're dead. You're *both* dead."

A dark shadow appeared behind Porter. A shadow he didn't see, but I did. Finally, he was here.

"What a shame," Detective Murphy said. "All this for a couple of wiped flash drives."

Porter whipped around, his eyes zeroing in on the team of officers who had entered the room, guns pointed at him.

Murphy looked at Finch, then at Blunt. "Call 9-1-1."

Blunt nodded.

Murphy placed a hand on Finch's shoulder. "Where'd he hit you?"

"Chest. I feel okay. I've been through worse."

"I bet you have, son," Murphy said. "I bet you have."

Murphy turned to me. "Great work."

"I didn't get him to say everything you wanted him to say," I said.

"Close enough."

Porter looked at Murphy. "How did you know?"

"We've been tailing you and Chelsea ever since the day of Alexandra's funeral."

"So?"

"So, you and your daughter, you set this all up to make it look like Barbara did it," Murphy said. "And when Chelsea ditched the officer I assigned to her this morning, it was obvious we had our killer. And hey, if it makes you feel any better, there is *one* thing I believe."

"What's that?"

"The day Chelsea called and said she was being followed, I believe she was telling the truth, only *you* were the one doing the following, Porter."

Porter laughed. "How did you manage that theory?"

"When we processed the stolen car, the only evidence we found was a few hair fibers," Murphy said. "Turned out, they were synthetic, just like the synthetic hair Joss found on the cushion of your couch when she dropped by yesterday."

Porter was escorted out the front door, where I was waiting. I smiled as he passed me. "By the way, if you're wondering about Chelsea, don't worry. She's safe. She didn't make it too far before the cops grabbed her."

CHAPTER 55

THE NEXT DAY, I SAT ACROSS FROM CHELSEA IN A ROOM reserved for police questioning. The more I stared, the more I noticed she'd never reminded me more of the photos I'd seen of her real father than she did today. She looked haggard and frail. Sleep deprived. Detectives had been through one round of questioning already, trying to get her to confess. So far she'd refused to speak. At present, she wasn't speaking to me either.

"I'm flying home today," I said. "I wanted to see you before I left."

She responded with a shrug.

"Mind if I tell you a story?" I asked. "It's more of a theory, but I'd like to run it by you anyway."

Another shrug.

Tough crowd.

"I used to admire this writer. She was well known, respected. She was murdered one evening after a book signing, poisoned by her own daughter after the daughter discovered a secret her mother had been keeping from her all her life. At first it was hard for me to see the daughter as a suspect. I'd seen the agony in the daughter's eyes after learning what happened to her mother, and I didn't want to believe it was possible for her to do what she did. As the facts came out, I learned the writer was penning a memoir she hadn't told many people about. When news of the memoir started getting around, those affected by what the writer might say about them in her book began to worry."

I paused then said, "How am I doing so far?"

"How would I know? It's your story. Not mine."

"Like all good stories, this one has a twist. See, even after the police figured out the daughter was responsible for her mother's death, the daughter still didn't confess to killing her mother. The man who raised her said he did it, even though I knew he didn't. But he loved her enough to do it anyway. Doesn't seem fair, does it?"

She remained silent.

I layered in a dose of reality, made it personal.

"Here's what I believe happened, Chelsea. You poisoned your mother with pesticide you stole from one of your fiancé's parents' ranches. The day he came with you to my hotel, I noticed he had a bit of hay stuck beneath his right shoe. I asked Detective Murphy to check out where Bradley's parents' wealth came from. Because of the Claiborness's political affiliations, he didn't need to check them out. They're well known here. He told me the Claibornes own several ranches in this state. Turns out fluoroacetate is used to control the predators on their farms, so naturally, it would be easy for you to get your hands on it, and you did."

She lowered her head. I kept going.

"Once your mother was dead, you must have told Porter what you did. Not at first, I don't think. I'm guessing you did it after I broke into your house looking for the flash drive. It scared you, and even though you were angry with him just like you were at your mother, you confessed, and he tried to help you cover it up the only way he knew how—by leading police to believe someone else did it, so the focus wouldn't be on either one of you. He also wanted to contain the fact you were Elias's daughter, and that's why he wanted the flash drive. He didn't know whether Alexandra wrote about you in her book or not, but he wasn't taking any chances. And if he could get his hands on it before Barbara did, he could contain it. While I admire his love for you, his plan wasn't well thought out."

"I didn't do anything," she said. "You can't prove anything."

"But you did, Chelsea. You were angry. Not just because she lied, and not just because she wasn't the kind of mother she should have been, but because if your secret got out, not only would the world see you differently, the people around you would see you differently. Bradley. Bradley's parents."

I reached across the table, grabbed her hand. "My story might not be one-hundred-percent accurate, but I'll bet it's close. Whatever happens now, I want you to know one thing. Even after what you've done, you're not your mother, and you're not Elias Pratt. One of the best ways you can prove that to yourself and to everyone else is to tell the truth."

I slid the chair back, stood, and walked to the door.

"Hey."

I turned back. "Yeah?"

"Interesting story. Too bad it's not true."

I shrugged. "What do I know? I'm just a writer."

CHAPTER 56

One Week Later

I FIDGETED WITH MY SKIRT, FIGHTING MY INNER URGE to grab it, pull it down a couple more inches or find a pair of scissors and cut it off. I despised skirts almost as much as I despised dresses and all manner of dressy things. What fun was an outfit if it didn't offer some breathing room, or the kind of fabric that could be washed in a regular old washing machine when it got dirty?

To get my mind off my choice of attire for the day, I thought of Chelsea. Murphy had called me a few days before to say she'd done the right thing, and after three grueling days of interrogations, she'd confessed to her crimes, admitting to poisoning her mother and attempting to poison Barbara Berry. One thing she didn't admit was Porter's part in it. No matter. He'd done a stupendous job of incriminating himself the night he was arrested.

Murphy still found it hard to believe that both flash drives were empty. Truth was, they weren't. I suspected the one Barbara planned on exchanging for a wad of cash was just a prop. The one I'd taken from Alex's house, I wiped clean, deciding Roland was right when he said some things in life didn't need to be revealed. Whether or not the manuscript itself was still out there somewhere, only time would tell.

Finch had glanced at me several times over the past two minutes, probably wondering what had me so self-absorbed that I'd abruptly stopped the conversation we'd been having.

He parked the car, walked over to me, and offered me his arm. I'd never been the damsel in distress type, but I was out of my element in a skirt and heels so I took it anyway.

"You look beautiful," he said. "Don't be nervous."

Before I could utter something stupidly sarcastic, he pulled open the chapel door. My eyes darted around, hoping for an empty row in the back so I could slip in unnoticed. My wishful thinking soon ended when my mother's eyes locked on mine.

The second she saw me, she shot out of her seat in the second row and speed-walked in my direction. She threw her arms around me and squealed, causing all those in attendance to look at us. "I knew you'd come, Joslyn! I just knew it!"

"Hi, Mom."

She planted a kiss on my cheek and pointed in the direction she'd just come from. "I saved you a seat."

"It doesn't look like there's enough room for both of us, so we're just going to sit in the back."

"Nonsense! You never said Finchie was coming with you, but that's all right. We can all squish in right next to your brother and sister."

My sister, whose personality was a mirror image to my mother, smiled and waved, furthering the interest of all the gawkers in the room. My brother smirked like he was all too happy to let me endure a little fresh hell for a change. In my mind, I rewound myself back to when I'd stepped on the plane bound for Salt Lake City, back to the moment I'd made the decision to make the trip in the first place.

Sensing my discomfort, Finch tried to alleviate the tight seating situation by saying, "It's just fine, ma'am. I'll wait back here until it's over."

"I'll sit back here too," I said.

"You won't either." She tugged my shirt sleeve, leading the way to the second row.

My brother cupped a hand over his mouth, attempting to control his laughter. Finch, thinking he was free to do as he pleased, Finch stepped into an aisle in the back row only to be scolded by my mother when she turned around. Five squished minutes later, the wedding ceremony between my cousin and my ex's brother began. Twenty minutes after that, it was over, and I was successfully outside and free, or so I thought.

The sound of Lucas's boots pounding the asphalt surface as he chased after me derailed my plans for a quick getaway. "Joss, wait up. Just a second. Stop. Will you stop, please?"

My head said to keep going, but my heart disagreed, and just this once I listened.

I stopped. Finch stopped too, his feet spread apart, arms folded in front of his chest.

"Why are you leaving so soon?" Lucas asked. "You just got here."

"I came for the wedding. It's over."

"Stay a while. At least for the reception tonight."

"It's better if I go."

"Who's it better for? You?"

"Why do you want me to stay, Lucas?" I asked.

"I haven't seen you in ages. I thought we could catch up."

"Why? Because we have history? Because we were married? Because we had a daughter together? You don't know me anymore, Lucas. You *knew* me. That woman, the one you married, she no longer exists. Nothing you can say or do now can ever bring her back."

"Joss, come on. Hear me out."

Knowing Finch was close to stepping in, I flattened a hand, held it out in his direction. "No. I was done hearing anything you had to say the day Elena died."

"Why? Because you'd rather pretend like she hadn't existed? Is it easier for you, because it sure as hell isn't as easy for me."

"Don't talk about Elena. You don't get to talk about her. Not to me."

"Maybe we need to talk about her. Maybe it's time."

"I choose to live my life for today, not yesterday," I said. "If yesterday is where you want to live, that's your choice."

Lucas glanced at Finch. "Look, man. Can you give us a minute here?"

Finch looked at me. I smiled and nodded, and he backed away. Not far, but far enough.

Voice lowered, Lucas leaned toward me. "I know you'll never be able to forgive me for what happened, but there's nothing I can do about it. I can't take it back. If I could, I would. I should have been a better husband to you. I should have shown you the respect you deserved. If I had, everything would be different."

His eyes filled with tears. Except for the night Elena died, he'd never been emotional in front of me before.

"I still love you, Joss. I'll always love you."

His heartfelt words appealed to the younger version of me, and just for a moment, I saw the boy I fell in love with in high school. I reached out, squeezed his hand. "We had some great memories, Lucas, and a beautiful daughter together. But, you have to let her go now, and let me go. Find someone who makes you happy."

He stood for a moment, then nodded. "It was good seeing you."

I smiled. "Take care of yourself, okay?"

CHAPTER 57

One hour later

I KNELT IN FRONT OF A HEADSTONE, PLACING THE colorful flowers against it. I brushed a hand across an oval portrait of a young, sweet-faced girl. My sweet girl. Part of me wanted to claw my fingers into the rich earth, crawl inside, and wrap my arms around her, joining her in eternal rest. I would give anything to run my hands through her silken hair one last time, hear a single syllable from her melodic voice, hold her in my arms again.

I wiped a tear from my eyelid, waved Finch over. "I want to tell you something."

"Joss, you don't have to—"

"I was driving, coming back a day early from a trip to my aunt's house in St. George, Utah. Elena was in the back in her car seat. She was three years old. We had the music going. We were singing and laughing. My cell phone rang. I didn't answer it, didn't even look to see who was calling. I never answered my phone while I was driving. A minute later, it rang again. Then again two minutes after that. The person called four times in six minutes. I thought it was an emergency, so the next time, I answered it."

"Who was calling?" Finch asked.

"My cousin Courtney."

"The one who got married today?"

I nodded.

"She was upset," I said. "Yelling into the phone. I couldn't understand her."

"What was she upset about?"

"She kept saying, 'I have to tell you something. Don't be mad at me, okay? Promise you won't be upset with me when I tell you.' I told her I was driving, asked if it could wait until I got home. We were so close. Ten more minutes and I'd be there."

"What did she say?"

"She'd driven by my house earlier that day, saw my friend's car there. She knew I was out of town and found it odd my friend would stop by when I wasn't at home. Two hours later, my cousin drove by again. The car was still there. Courtney parked up the street, crept up to the window in front of the house, peeked inside. Lucas was naked on the sofa with my best friend, both of them all tangled up in each other."

Finch bent down, placed a hand on my shoulder. "I've been through it myself. I'm sorry."

"When Courtney told me what she saw, I was furious. The more she talked, the madder I became. I ended the call with her and called him."

"Did he admit it to you?"

"He did. Honestly, he had no choice. When my cousin saw them together, she stormed into the house. He begged her not to tell me, and I think he hadn't called because he was waiting around to see if she'd do it."

"What did he say when you confronted him?"

"He asked how I felt about it, how I was doing. I kept thinking about our marriage, about how everything was fine one minute and the next it was over. I wasn't speeding, but it was dark outside, and my eyes were so filled with tears I couldn't see the road. The lines all blended together. In the midst of all that, Lucas was still yacking away."

"I can't imagine how difficult that was for you."

We locked eyes, and I knew he knew what I was about to say was far more difficult than anything I'd already said. "I wanted to pull off the road, but I couldn't. There were miles and miles of orange cones on the side of the road because of the construction, and the other lane was blocked off. One of the cones blew onto the highway. By the time I swerved, it was too late. The side of my car smacked into it. I jerked the steering wheel, and my car slipped off the freeway into the ditch. I can still hear the sound of Elena screaming."

Finch took my hand in his.

"My head cracked against the steering wheel before the airbag deployed, and I blacked out," I said. "When I came to, lights flashed all around me. I was inside an ambulance. I lifted my head, tried to see Elena. I asked one of the medics to bring me to her. As long as I live, I'll never forget the look on the medic's face when the officer walked over and told me Elena was dead."

Silence passed between us for a moment, then Finch spoke. "I have witnessed death in all its forms. Even when it had to be done or couldn't be avoided, I never found peace in it. You choose how you let it change you. What happened to your daughter was an accident. You can grieve, and you can hold on to all the good times, but you can't stop living."

"You're right," I said. "Some days I feel numb, like adrenaline pumping through my veins is the only thing that's keeping me alive. Other days, I feel fine."

"And today?"

"Today I feel blessed to have you in my life. I know I haven't said it, Finch, but it means a lot to me that I can talk to you."

He stretched out his hand, helping me get back on my feet. "You can always talk to me. I will always be here for you."

"I know you will."

"Ready to go say goodbye to your parents and head out?"

Two hours ago, I would have jumped at the offer. Now I realized there was only one way to face things. "Yeah, let's stop there, and after, let's stop at the church again. There's a reception I'd like to go to."

THE END

ABOUT CHERYL BRADSHAW

Cheryl Bradshaw is a *New York Times* and *USA Today* bestselling author. She currently has two series: Sloane Monroe mystery/thriller series and the Addison Lockhart paranormal suspense series. Stranger in Town (Sloane Monroe series #4) was a 2013 Shamus Award finalist for Best PI Novel of the Year, and I Have a Secret (Sloane Monroe series #3) was a 2013 eFestival of Words winner for best thriller novel.

BOOKS BY
CHERYL BRADSHAW

Sloane Monroe Series

Black Diamond Death
Murder in Mind
I Have a Secret
Stranger in Town
Bed of Bones
Flirting With Danger (Novella)
Hush Now Baby
Dead of Night (Novella)
Gone Daddy Gone

Addison Lockhart Series

Grayson Manor Haunting
Rosecliff Manor Haunting

Maisie Fezziwig Series

Hickory Dickory Dead

Till Death do us Part Short Story Series
Whispers of Murder
Echoes of Murder

Stand-Alone Novels
Eye for Revenge
The Devil Died at Midnight